Pl

C000101217

Pleasure Hunt

SOPHIE DANSON

BLACK
lace

First published in 1993 by
Black Lace
332 Ladbroke Grove
London W10 5AH

Typeset by CentraCet, Cambridge
Printed and bound by Cox & Wyman Ltd, Reading,
Berks

ISBN 0 35232 880 0

Black Lace novels are sexual fantasies. In real life,
always practise safe sex.

Chapter One

The young man's hands were broad and strong, like a bear's paws, and Olympia shivered with pleasure as the muscular fingers ran over her body, awakening her desire. His lips were on hers, his tongue pushing its way into the warm cavern of her mouth, and she returned his kiss willingly, hungry for his sex.

She reached out and touched him, shivering with satisfaction as she traced the thick, firm outline beneath his pants. He was big. She would enjoy taking him inside her.

She glanced around her, anxious that they should not be disturbed. As she had planned, the lift was securely jammed between floors; it was sure to take a good half hour for the engineers to get it going again. Plenty of time for a little *ad hoc* fun.

Freeing herself from his encircling arms, Olympia slid down his body and deftly tugged down his trouser zip. He opened his mouth – doubtless

1

to protest, since a man like him would be accustomed to making love to his partners *his* way – and then gasped as he felt Olympia's wicked fingers sneak into his pants and pull out his erect hardness.

'You look good, *chéri*,' whispered Olympia, stroking his shaft with delicate precision. 'And you feel good. Now let's see if you taste good, too.'

She examined her trophy with pleasure, noting that although it was not much above average length, the flesh was very thick and firm. As she savoured the first, thrilling taste of him, she wondered if she would have room inside her for all of this magnificent prize. He groaned as her lips closed around him, and he clutched at her head, stroking her hair convulsively and moaning in an unintelligible patois.

What did it matter if Olympia couldn't understand his words? She was not here to make polite conversation. She ran her tongue around the tip of the young man's manhood, and was rewarded with the salty taste of slippery sex-fluid, oozing from the tip. Though she wanted him desperately, she wouldn't hurry this part of the game. She wanted to enjoy playing with him – just enough to drive him crazy with lust, and make him really ready for her.

She slid her hand down his shaft and cupped the twin globes that nestled so prettily between his thighs. They were deliciously heavy in her palm, full of promise as some juicy tropical fruit. The thought made her so excited that a familiar warm wetness made its presence felt between her thighs. Already her love-mound was throbbing with the expectation of passion.

Olympia's tongue teased the young man for a little while longer, as she amused herself by taking him to the brink of pleasure, only to keep him there until the anticipation of orgasm became unbearable. Again and again she refused to grant him release in her mouth, though he tried desperately to bring himself to his longed-for climax. His distress did not worry Olympia. The longer the game went on, the more he would savour his pleasure when she finally did take pity on him.

At last, sensing that her young lover was nearing the point of exhaustion, Olympia released him from her mouth. His engorged flesh was glistening with saliva, mingled with his own clear sex-juice. He stared at her desperately, despairingly. Surely this crazy, predatory, irresistible Englishwoman didn't intend leaving him like this?

'*Alors, regarde-moi,*' Olympia commanded him. 'Just look what I have for you.'

Getting to her feet, she hitched up her pencil skirt to reveal a pair of red lace panties, cut very high in the leg and so skimpy that they allowed a few tendrils of auburn hair to escape from the edges. Swiftly, Olympia pulled down her panties and stepped out of them. With an impish grin, she wiped them across the young man's face, passing the damp, fragrant crotch under his nose. He closed his eyes and groaned as he breathed in her scent.

'*Un p'tit cadeau pour toi, Jean-Jacques.*'

Then, bracing her back against the wall of the lift, Olympia parted her thighs and slipped a hand between them, delicately opening up the flower of her sex so that the young lift attendant had the full benefit of her moist pleasure-garden. She smiled

3

shamelessly as she began stroking the intimate folds of her flesh. Now she was really going to enjoy teasing him . . .

She pleasured herself with an artless grace, revelling in the young man's lustful, yet disconsolate gaze as she obliged him to watch her playing with herself in front of him. She knew how much he longed to throw this impudent little hussy to the floor and take her, but something was holding him back. It wasn't difficult to guess what it was. After all, Mademoiselle was a favoured guest in this prestigious Paris hotel, and he was just an insignificant employee. One adverse word from Olympia Deschamps, and this fine young fellow would get his marching orders.

And yet, if only he could see into her heart, he would know how groundless his fears were. All she wanted was for them to enjoy a little pleasure together. Still, it was good to feel her ascendancy over this young man, who was so accustomed to having everything his own way. It would do him no harm to subject himself, for once in his vigorous young life, to the demands and desires of a woman.

By now the poor boy was round-eyed with frustration. He slipped a hand down to touch himself but Olympia shook her head sternly, and prised away his fingers.

'Non. C'est interdit, tu comprends? I forbid it! C'est pour tout à l'heure, you understand? Later. Save yourself for me; it will be worth it, I promise you!'

Olympia leant against the back wall of the lift, running gentle, skilful fingertips across the erect buds of her breasts as she rubbed herself to slow, luxurious pleasure. A glance between her half-

4

closed eyelids confirmed that the youth's gaze was desperate, dog-like. Well, perhaps it was time to throw him a succulent tit-bit.

'*Alors, suce-moi – tu veux*?' She grinned. '*Lèche-moi*. Show me what you can do with your tongue, Jean-Jacques.'

The young man was not slow in responding to the challenge. Throwing himself at her feet with a sob of relief, he pressed his eager face against the hot, moist flesh between her thighs. It was late afternoon and his face was rough, his hard stubble pricked the tender flesh of her womanhood. She shivered with the delicious discomfort of it.

'*Doucement*, gently now.'

But Olympia was loving every minute of it; revelling in the clumsy eagerness of the young man's caresses. This young puppy might think he knew all there was to know about making love to a woman, but if truth were told he was a rough and ready lover. No one, it seemed, had ever taught him the niceties of love-making; the little tricks that please a woman and make her hot and wet and hungry for sex. Well, he must now become a pupil, under Olympia's expert tuition.

Olympia caught hold of his hands and guided them gently but firmly, showing him how to pleasure her.

'There – that's it. Touch me there. Tease me with your fingertips, as gently as if you were stroking the petals of a flower. Now, flick the tip of your tongue across me . . . oh, yes! Now bite my bud, but oh so gently . . . aah!'

So eager was her pupil that Olympia felt dizzy, her excitement approaching all too quickly. Such a pity, she had hoped to make their encounter last a little longer. Ah well, it was of no account. There would be other pleasures, in other places, and with other lovers. And besides, there was still this eager young stallion to please. She was far too polite to send him home with hunger in his eyes.

And so, Olympia abandoned herself to the familiar waves of pleasure; to the creeping, surging warmth that began somewhere deep in her belly, and made her thighs ache and tingle with the anticipation of delight.

'Oh . . . yes! Hold me . . .'

Spreading her thighs as wide as she could, she pressed her back against the wall of the lift and opened herself utterly to Jean-Jacques' probing tongue. Its muscular tip flicked back and forth across her labia, sliding the hood of her clitoris across its hypersensitive head. She was coming, coming, coming . . .

'Ah, Jean-Jacques!'

She clutched at his head as the orgasm swept over her, pressing his face harder and harder against her mound; prolonging and intensifying the pleasure. Wet trickles of love-juice oozed out of her and into Jean-Jacques' mouth. He lapped up every drop delightedly like a greedy animal.

Still weak and dazed with pleasure, Olympia allowed herself to slide down the wall until her backside was touching the carpeted floor and her knees were spread wide, displaying the glistening, red heart of her sex. Her burning throbbing need for love had not yet been quite satisfied, and she was eager for a second journey into ecstasy, maybe even a third; who could tell how many? For Olympia Deschamps was a very unusual young woman:

a woman who had decided to dedicate her life to the arts and pleasures of love.

The carpeted floor was rough, and it gave her an uncomfortable, yet undeniably arousing, sensation as her buttocks parted and rubbed against the harsh woollen pile. The delicate membranes of her sex responded instantly to this delicious new stimulus, and she reached out her arms to Jean-Jacques.

'*Prends-moi*; take me, take me now!'

The youth needed no second bidding. Taking hold of her by the waist he slid her down further until she was flat on her back on the floor, her skirt up round her waist and her bare buttocks crushed against the rough carpeting. He was by no means a stylish lover; but there was a certain raw excitement in the eager way he laid her down and aimed his love-dart at the opening of her sex.

Jean-Jacques thrust into her hungrily, and she let out a little gasp of pleasure; he was beautfully hard, and she was glad now that she had made him wait so long for her. He would not last long, but then, neither would she. Aroused as she was, the merest touch on her love-button would spark her into ferocious, orgasmic life.

She wrapped her legs around his waist and moved in time to his thrusts, answering each movement of his powerful hips with a corresponding thrust of her tight backside. The rough floor covering abraded the delicate flesh between her buttocks quite delightfully, and she welcomed the slight discomfort, which only served to augment the delicious warmth already spreading through her loins for the second time.

'*J'arrive, j'arrive!*' gasped Jean-Jacques, and

Olympia felt him stiffen inside her, a second before he poured forth his tribute. The simple thought of his hot, white seed jetting into her was enough to trigger Olympia's second access of pleasure, and she clutched him convulsively as her spasms rose to meet his foaming tide of love-juice.

Just as the pleasure was ebbing away, and Olympia was considering what they might do next to pass the time agreeably, there was a whirring and grinding of machinery, and the lights flickered as the lift-cage creaked and clanked back into life.

'Hein. Merde!' muttered Jean-Jacques, leaping to his feet in a terrible panic, and making ineffectual attempts to tidy himself up.

Perfectly unruffled, Olympia got up from the floor, dusted herself down and slid her skirt back over her thighs. Her fragrant panties, she rescued from the handle of the lift door and stuffed deftly into her handbag. A quick brush of her long red-gold hair, and she looked unquestionably respectable. Only her flushed cheeks betrayed the fact that something very Gallic had just taken place between a lift attendant and a remarkable young Englishwoman.

Jean-Jacques was looking thoroughly flustered as the lift sank towards the ground floor. Olympia planted a playful kiss on the tip of his shaft, and popped it neatly back into his pants, zipping and buttoning him as though he were a child.

'There!' she smiled. 'No one will ever know. *Personne*! If you don't want them to.'

At that very moment, the lift cage reached the ground floor, and the doors slid open with an electric hum. Without so much as a backward glance, Olympia strode out into the foyer of the

8

Hôtel St Germain. She gave only the briefest thought to the passengers who were flocking noisily into the lift, and wondered vaguely what they would make of that damp, white stain on the burgundy carpet.

'Ah. Mademoiselle Deschamps! All is well, I trust. I am so very sorry about the lift – such a thing has never happened before! But your room is to your satisfaction, *oui*? I selected it for you myself. Such a pretty view from your window.'

The flushed face of the desk clerk amused Olympia as she placed her order for a morning newspaper. She wondered if he would be half so concerned, were she not a stunning red-blonde with emerald eyes, never-ending legs and an enviable pair of breasts. Could he, she wondered, smell the scent of her brief encounter in the lift? It was an intriguing thought, and a little half-smile crept across her face. Perhaps later, if she should find herself at a loose end . . .

'Yes, thank you. For the most part the room is excellent. But unfortunately, the shower isn't working properly. Could you send someone up to fix it as soon as possible, please?'

'Most certainly, Mademoiselle. My deepest apologies. Would you perhaps like us to move you to a different room?'

'No, thank you; that won't be necessary. I'm going up to my room to rest now. *A tout à l'heure, M'sieur.*'

She turned on her heel and retraced her steps to the lift, making sure to accentuate the natural sway of her hips for the benefit of the desk clerk. He would surely have the shower repaired more promptly if he was lusting hopelessly for her.

9

Her room was 618, on the sixth floor. It did indeed have a nice view – a parade of smart boutiques and the distant Bois de Boulogne – but Olympia was not in Paris to look at the sights. As she got undressed and lay down on the bed, she thought of the quest which filled her every waking moment, and drove her on with a burning determination. She would succeed – no matter what the cost.

Despite her exotic name, Olympia Deschamps had been born and brought up in England, the daughter of an English mother and a French father. Her mother had died when Olympia was a small child, and she had been brought up by her father, Olivier, a successful banker, famous in England as a man of culture and a philanthropist. But the late Olivier Deschamps' fame owed less to his financial acumen than to a more unusual skill: for Monsieur Deschamps was a dedicated sexual adventurer, the consort of princesses and the lover of sensual women everywhere. Courteous, sensitive and skilful in the arts of love, Olivier Deschamps was accepted in the best society and not one of his conquests had ever been anything but complimentary about him.

But, for all his successes in love, Olivier Deschamps had one secret sadness: a failure which he confided to only one person – his daughter, Olympia.

In the arrogance of his youth, Olivier Deschamps had believed he could do anything. And when he heard of the legendary Légion d'Amour, he knew that he must, at all costs, join its ranks. No one ever openly admitted to membership of the Légion – for its activities were shrouded in the

10

darkest secrecy – but it was said that the Légionnaires were the most skilful and adventurous lovers in the world. They were so dedicated to their art that, if necessary, they would die for it.

Olivier's life was utterly transformed as soon as he discovered the mysterious Légion. All at once, his life had been given a new purpose: somehow, he had to track down this secret fraternity, and beg to undergo the arduous trials necessary to become a member.

Ten years he spent in his quest; and then, finally, his dream came true. One night, in North Africa, he was approached by a masked figure in Bedouin robes, who asked him if still wished to join the Légion d'Amour. He was given seven tasks to complete – acts of sexual potency, ingenuity and resilence which would daunt any ordinary mortal.

Six of the tasks, he completed with honour and aplomb. The seventh, he failed. Cast out into the desert, he never again heard from the Légion. For in the Légion d'Amour there are no second chances.

He never recovered from the pain of failure. There were some who said that Olivier Deschamps died of a broken heart.

One day, young Olympia sat at his feet, listening to her father's tales of his sexual conquests, and of the time when he so nearly became a member of the Légion.

'One day, Father, I shall join the Légion d'Amour,' announced Olympia, with all the certainty of youth. 'I shall join, and you shall be proud of me.'

But Olivier shook his head.

'My dear child, you are brave and spirited. But

11

you must empty your mind of such foolish dreams. No woman has ever been admitted to the ranks of the Légion d'Amour.

Olympia fixed him with her bright emerald eyes. 'Then I shall be the first,' she declared.

And so it was, that, ten years later, Olympia Deschamps found herself in a luxurious Paris hotel, waiting and hoping for the chance she craved. It was rumoured that the Légion had its headquarters in Paris. Perhaps, after so many attempts, she would be lucky. Perhaps this time she would be called.

'Wait, and watch, and listen,' he father had told her, only weeks before he died, 'And be patient. The Légion will summon you if you are ready. If not, you must simply keep on waiting.'

That was easier said than done, mused Olympia, who was not good at waiting. When she saw something she wanted, she generally moved heaven and earth to get it. Especially when that something was sex. She adored sex, and since men adored her, she could steadily pursue her favourite hobby. Over the past few years, her job as agent for an international art dealer had left her plenty of time between business assignments to enjoy the pleasurable things of life. She felt certain that she was now ready to meet any sexual challenge which the Légion could throw at her. Why, oh why, had they not yet contacted her? This was her third visit to Paris in as many months, and still no word from them.

Ah well, there was always work to keep her occupied. Tomorrow, she had an appointment at a little private gallery on the Ile St Louis, where she had occasionally picked up some interesting pieces by unknown artists at a knockdown price. But until then, what was a girl to do?

She ran her hands over her body, mentally reliving her encounter with the handsome young lift attendant, and his oh-so-eager body. He had been fun. She wished he were here now, with his rippling muscles and the obliging hardness bulging from his pants. He had tasted good, so good, on her tongue. How she longed to have him in her mouth again; to feel the exquisite power of knowing that a man's pleasure was between her skilful lips, choosing the exact moment when she would release him into a sunburst of coloured lights and an outpouring of opalescent delight.

Instinctively, she slipped a hand between her legs and let her thighs relax. The scent of her last encounter rose up from her pleasure mound, reinforcing memories of the afternoon's frolics in the lift. Her right hand strayed to her breast, and began toying with the nipple. She had incredibly sensitive nipples, large and fleshy. They loved to be touched, caressed, kissed. Even the touch of a light summer breeze could arouse them into wakeful crests, ready for passion.

Olympia slipped her finger between her love-lips and toyed for a while with the hot, sticky wetness that betrayed her former and future pleasure. For she was growing wet all over again; oozing with moisture that simply begged for a lover to fill her up, to slide in and out of her, paying homage to her tight, eager womanhood.

She felt for her clitoris, and shivered with pleasure as her finger tip brushed across the little bud. It was hard and throbbing, and very ready for the fray. As she rubbed it, Olympia wondered what it would feel like to have her clitoris pierced; to have a tiny silver ring through the head of this most sensitive heart of her womanhood. A friend from her eastern meditation class had had hers pierced, and had told her that the sensations were exquisite, unparalleled. Well, that was one more adventure yet to experience. Perhaps, when she got back to England, she would give it a try.

Right now, pleasure awaited. Pleasure welling up like a spring, deep in the heart of her. Pleasure that made her breath come in short, sharp gasps, keeping time with the accelerating rhythm of her fingers, playing skilfully with the rose-pink bud between her love-lips.

A wonderful, hot hardness. Thrusting in and out of her. A thick, firm manhood, and big, full globes of flesh slapping against her backside. How she longed for an endless night of love, during which there were no limits, no boundaries that could not be crossed. She would beg for mercy, but her relentless lover would pay no heed to her pleas. He had become her master and she would be his steed. He would just keep on riding her. Riding her through the night, until dawn.

'Y-a-t'il quelqu'un? Ah, Mademoiselle!'

Olympia's eyes snapped open and she turned her head in shock, to see a figure standing in the doorway. A man, dark and stocky, perhaps in his mid-thirties, was standing half in and half out of the room, with one hand on the door handle and the other holding a large canvas bag of tools. On this hot July day, he appeared to be naked except for espadrilles and a pair of blue denim bib-and-brace overalls.

So, this must be the shower repair man! Olympia's eyes narrowed as she took him in, appraising him from head to toe. Hmm . . . nice, tight bum. Broad shoulders and muscular arms. Not particularly tall, but the huge bulge in the front of his overalls looked extremely promising. Maybe she wasn't going to be at a loose end this afternoon, after all.

'*Oh, Mademoiselle, je m'excuse. Je croyais qu'il n'y avait personne dans la chambre.* I will leave—'

'No, no! It's all right, really it is. *Pas de problème.* Come in. Let me show you what's wrong with the shower. C'*est la douche – comprenez*?'

She got up off the bed slowly, making sure that the handsome young Frenchman had ample opportunity to feast his eyes on her naked body – not that he hadn't already. She wondered just how long he'd been standing there, watching her summoning up her own pleasure. Picking up a silky bathrobe from the bedside chair, she made a half-hearted attempt to cover herself up. But the robe had no belt, and with each step forward she took, it swung open, revealing the ample curve of her bosom, long, silky thighs and a triangle of glossy red-gold curls.

Olympia cast a sly glance at the repair man. He was swallowing nervously, and gripping his toolbox so tightly that his knuckles were turning white. Olympia couldn't help thinking how those strong hands might feel gripping her thighs, lifting her up and crushing her to that firm, muscular body.

'In here, Monsieur.' She led the way into the semi-gloom of the windowless private bathroom, making sure that, as they passed through the door, her silk-clad backside pressed fleetingly against the

15

front of the young man's overalls. She had not been mistaken. He was hot, hard and throbbing for her.

But he was shy. She could tell he was afraid to make that crucial first move. Well, if she wanted him, Olympia Deschamps would just have to think of some way to break the ice.

She slid open the door of the shower cubicle, and leant over to switch on the water, knowing only too well that the silk bathrobe would fall open, revealing a shapely breast with a golden tan that spoke volumes about the many happy hours Olympia Deschamps had spent naked in the sunshine.

She turned on the tap, but nothing happened.

'You see? No water. It's broken. *Cassé. Ne marche pas.* Can you do anything?'

The workman nodded.

'I think . . . I try.'

He squatted down on his haunches with his toolbox, opened it and rummaged around for a plumber's wrench. Olympia shivered delightedly as she looked down at his mop of curly brown hair, the little hairs on the back of his nut-brown neck, the broad shoulders with the muscles that rippled, just beneath the surface of the golden skin. She longed to touch, to kiss, to caress . . .

Unable to restrain herself, she reached out and let her fingers play, very gently, on the nape of his neck. His flesh was hot, dry, vibrant, like a lizard's that has slept all day in the sun and has only come out into the cool of the night, to hunt.

He started at the gentleness of her touch, and looked up, questioningly. Olympia smiled; a strange light burned in his dark brown eyes, and she knew he understood.

The workman got to his feet, seemingly forgetting what had just passed between them, and began fiddling with the tap that turned on the shower. Olympia was in the grip of a terrible frustration. She wanted to pounce on him, tear off his clothes, force him to make love to her, but that would spoil everything. He might be shy, but she sensed that this young man knew instinctively how to play the game of love.

'*Le robinet.*' He turned to Olympia and explained. '*C'est coincé.* He is . . . how you say? . . . jam?'

'Jammed. The tap is jammed?'

'*Oui, c'est ça.* The tap, he is jammed. He will not turn far enough. And so you have no water.'

'Can you mend it?'

'*Hein, oui . . . j'crois.* I will try.'

As he worked away at the shower, Olympia looked on with unadulterated lust in her heart. She eyed him longingly; the way he moved was poetic, the graceful strength of those muscles. He must be a body builder; he had such a wonderfully tight backside.

After an eternity, he stood back and folded his arms in triumph.

'*Et voilà!*'

'You've mended it? Oh, thank you!'

Olympia felt a thank-you kiss was in order, and obliged with a celebratory peck on the cheek, her right hand taking advantage of the close contact to slide down his body and give his nice tight bum a subtle but appreciative squeeze.

Extricating himself from her grasp, the repair man reached over and turned on the shower.

17

Warm water cascaded out, filling the room with steam. It was a hot day; a cold shower would be more appropriate, thought Olympia, particularly in view of the rising temperature of her lust. Still, she did need a shower, and it seemed such a pity to waste all that water.

Artfully, she slipped her robe off her shoulders, and let it fall to the ground. The workman watched, dumbstruck, his brown eyes protruding as if they were on stalks. He must have been all of twenty-five, but he looked like a guilty schoolboy, seeing his first naked woman and wondering if the headmistress was going to come along any moment and catch him peeping. So much for Gallic Lotharios, though Olympia, with a little chuckle.

'I really must try it,' she explained. *'Je vais l'essayer.'*

And she stepped into the shower cubicle. The plumber stood and stared, unable to make up his mind whether he should stay and enjoy the floor show, or make his apologies and leave. He had never met a woman quite like Olympia Deschamps before.

It was so cleverly executed that no one would ever have guessed it was not an accident. Olympia stumbled so prettily as she reached for the shower gel that even she almost believed she had not done it deliberately. As she had hoped, the young repair man leapt forward to her aid.

'Mademoiselle!'

He was behind her now, and his hands were around her waist, supporting her. They were trembling with suppressed desire, and she responded instantly to his touch, taking his hands and moving them upwards until they rested on the swell of her breasts.

'*Belle; très, très belle,*' he murmured in her ear, and began kissing the nape of her neck, very gently, as he kneaded the firm, golden flesh of her breasts. They stepped further into the shower, and he reached out for the tap, turning it on full, so that the steaming water cascaded over their flesh like a tropical waterfall.

Olympia leant back against him, her naked backside pressed up against his burgeoning hardness, insistent through the sodden fabric of his overalls. She reached behind her, and began stroking him through the wet denim, visualising him through her fingertips, enjoying the anticipation of his pleasure . . . and her own.

Her nipples were erect, and she could feel honey-sweet love juice oozing out of her, trickling from her love-lips to join the warm cascade of water down her inner thighs.

'*Déshabille-toi,*' she groaned, desperate with lust. 'Undress yourself for me, *je t'en prie.*'

Reluctantly he let go of her and stepped back. Instantly she missed the warm strength of his arms on her, holding her, pulling her towards him. She did not turn round, not wanting to spoil the moment when she would feel his nakedness against hers. Instead, she turned her face to the warm jet of water, closing her eyes and letting the water run down her face, her yearning breasts.

A few seconds later he was back, pulling her towards him with a gentle urgency.

'I want you,' he breathed.

'Give it to me . . .'

He pulled apart her buttocks, and she expected

19

to feel him thrusting into her; but he had other ideas. A bar of soap, well-lathered and slippery, slid between her thighs and began a sly, skilful movement backwards and forwards along the secret furrow of her womanhood. From clitoris to the delicate crease between her buttocks, this ingenious young lover tormented her most sensitive flesh. The perfumed soap stung a little, but the sensation was far from unpleasant. It heightened the throbbing of her sex-bud, and her entire body began to burn with desire for him.

All at once, he pushed the slippery bar of soap hard, and it disappeared right inside her, teasing and delighting her. Instinctively she clenched the muscles of her vagina, keeping the bar of soap inside her as her lover began manipulating her towards the peak of pleasure.

'Oh yes, yes! Give it to me quickly; give it to me, hard.'

He masturbated her expertly, one hand on her breast and the other on her clitoris, rubbing it with just the right degree of pressure; taking her to the glittering edge of pleasure again and again, until at last she could take no more.

Almost sobbing with relief, she reached orgasm. Her muscles tensed in a series of violent spasms, and a flood of slippery love-juice poured out from between her sex-lips, loosening the bar of soap and sending it slithering away into the drainage channel.

She slumped against him, panting, seemingly exhausted. But he was far from finished with her, and his ardour delighted Olympia. In a single, eager thrust he was inside her, his willing shaft parting her love-lips and entering the very heart of her womanhood.

Olympia sighed with satisfaction, and abandoned herself to all the wild delights of impromptu love-making.

Today was turning out to be quite entertaining, after all.

That evening, Olympia stretched out on her hotel bed and flicked half-heartedly through the TV channels. Some amateurish costume drama, badly dubbed from Spanish; game shows; interminable interviews with minor celebrities. French television hadn't improved since her last visit. Her diversions with the lift attendant and the shower repair man had passed the time agreeably, but that was hours ago. Olympia Deschamps was lonely, bored and once again hungry for love.

Then an item on the screen caught her eye. It was some sort of local magazine programme. She turned up the volume and listened.

'Tonight, at the Théâtre de la Timbale, controversial hypnotist Michel Laloupe is staging his late-night show, which has caused scandal and sensation in all the capitals of Europe. The performance begins at 11 o'clock and there are still a few tickets left, at 150 Francs . . .'

That's the one for me, thought Olympia, switching off the TV and bounding off the bed. That's where I'll go tonight.

Chapter Two

*T*he tiny Théâtre de la Timbale, in the heart of Montmartre, was thronged with excited theatregoers – young men and their giggly girlfriends, middle-aged couples looking for something a little different, and even a few aristocratic-looking men and their elegant wives, dripping with ostentatious jewellery. Michel Laloupe's late-night hypnotism show was already the talk of Paris.

Olympia paid her 150 Francs and went through the foyer into the auditorium. She was glad she wasn't too near the front. She'd heard what these hypnotists sometimes did to the people they lured up on to the stage. In fact, a friend of a friend had once been dragged out of the audience and made to think he was a chicken. She smiled at the memory and settled down in a comfortable seat, between a middle-aged matron and a thin young man in a tuxedo several sizes too big for him.

The light dimmed, the curtain duly rose and a fat, sweating compère bounced on to the stage and

22

told a string of blue jokes which produced nervous laughter. Olympia felt quite cheated, it was almost like being in an English working men's club. But the comedian gradually produced the desired effect; he warmed up the audience and relaxed them. Soon, a ripple of excitement ran round the room. Even Olympia felt a thrill of anticipation. What would the great Laloupe be like? Would he turn out to be a genius or a charlatan?

At last the house lights went down again, and Laloupe took the stage in a single brilliant white spotlight. Olympia found herself pleasantly surprised. Tall and very dark, with saturnine good looks, Michel Laloupe was very much aware of the effect he had upon his audience. Olympia noted for the first time that over half of the spectators were women. And they seemed instantly transfixed; perhaps he was already working his own brand of sexual magic on them.

The show began with a few innocent demonstrations of the hypnotic art. Olympia became vaguely bored. Where was all the scandal she had been led to expect? This was the sort of show you could take your maiden aunt to!

'And now,' announced Laloupe, 'it is time for the part of the show we have all been waiting for – the audience participation. My assistant Annick will call out the numbers of some seats within this auditorium. If your number is called, you must come up on stage.'

No fear, thought Olympia. If anyone has the cheek to call out my number, I shall just sit here and watch everybody else making a fool of themselves.

'*Rang G, soixante-quinze,*' announced the lovely

Annick – a petite brunette with a generous bosom and perfect smile.

A gale of laughter erupted on the other side of the theatre, and Olympia saw a middle-aged man being pushed to his feet by his family and friends. Red-faced but beaming, he made his way up the steps and on to the stage.

Michel Laloupe liked to toy with his victims. He knew exactly what his audience were expecting – something sleazy, something scandalous and, above all, something embarrassing. They had read the reviews, seen his television interviews. Well, they would have to wait a little while yet – but he was sure they would think it was worth the wait. He had screened the audience members as they entered the theatre, and selected his subjects with the utmost care. He did not think anyone would be going home disappointed.

Laloupe duly put the red-faced man into a deep trance without difficulty, got him to take off his jacket and shirt, and soon had him doing handstands and making farmyard noises. The audience enjoyed it, but they were restless, knowing that there was more – and better – to come. Others followed, a young girl who giggled incessantly until Laloupe hypnotised her and told her she was a tortoise. She was pretty quiet after that. Number followed number, and Olympia became so bored that she considered getting up and leaving.

'Rang T, siège trente-deux,' announced Annick, holding up a black card with golden writing on it. For a moment, Olympia did not realise that all eyes were on her. But before she knew it, hands were pushing her to her feet and she was walking mechanically down the aisle towards the stage.

24

Laloupe welcomed her with a satanic smile. Despite her legendary self-confidence, Olympia felt her legs buckle as their eyes met, and she almost fell into the hypnotist's arms. As she stumbled, she felt Laloupe's hand on her backside, probing, exploring, enjoying. Then it was gone, and she was standing beside him on the stage, telling herself that she would not, under any circumstances, allow herself to be hypnotised. No one was going to be in control of Olympia Deschamps' brain except Olympia herself!

'Relax,' a voice whispered, somewhere deep inside her head. 'Relax. You know you want to.'

It was strange because immediately the words entered her mind, Olympia felt an irresistible languor washing over her, making her feel weak, vulnerable and yet not the least bit afraid. Suddenly she realised that the eyes of every person in the theatre were on her, and she gave an involuntary giggle, revelling in her new-found celebrity status.

'Look at me, Olympia Deschamps. Look deep into my eyes.'

She stared, astonished that this man should know her name, and instinctively she looked up into Laloupe's face. Instantly her head began to swim, and she wanted to look away, but she could not. It was as though her gaze were locked to his, the bond indissoluble and iron-fast. And yet Laloupe's eyes were quite ordinary, a dull brown – she remembered that quite clearly from the publicity photographs on the foyer. But now they seemed to be burning with a brilliant green fire.

As she looked into Laloupe's eyes, Olympia felt images forming in her head. Images so seductive that, for a moment, she quite forgot where she was.

She saw a naked woman, dancing before a tall, dark man; his magnificent phallus hugely erect. There could be no mistaking the two figures; in the secret world of her mind, Olympia Deschamps was dancing naked for Michel Laloupe. A secret world no longer, for already it had been invaded by this skilful hypnotist. What other secrets, what other dreams and desires did he intent to plant in her head? She made a feeble attempt to resist, but it was useless – her body wanted to submit.

A faraway voice was speaking to the audience. It seemed light-years away, in another world.

'And now, *Messieurs-Dames*, a spectacle to delight and excite you. The delectable English Mademoiselle will perform the most intimate sensual acts for your entertainment and delectation.'

Olympia felt the cold, naked power of the man's voice – irresistible, smooth and sweet and never cloying. For some unaccountable, unfathomable reason, she knew that she wanted to serve this man – to become his plaything. All her resolve flew out of the window.

'Undress for me, Olympia. Undress for me alone. I command it.'

Although she knew she was baring her body to hundreds of people, Olympia felt as though she truly was undressing for Laloupe alone. His unique magnetism seemed to envelop her as she slipped off her jacket and unfastened the buttons on her thin, semi-diaphanous blouse. Then the sea-green skirt, it fell to the stage in a whispering sigh of raw silk. Underneath, she was wearing a thirties-style camiknicker in écru satin. She hesi-

26

tated, momentarily concious of the laughter, the gasps of lust and delighted disbelief.

'Remove it, Olympia. It is my very special wish to see you naked. Naked for me alone . . .'

She obeyed with an automatic ease, no guilt or fear clouding the perfect clarity of her mind. She was undressing for Laloupe. Laloupe was her master, and he wished to see her naked. The rightness of the command was unquestionable.

Pulling down the shoulder straps, she stepped daintily out of the seductive underwear. Naked, save for her stockings and high heels, Olympia stood on the stage, awaiting her master's next command. The coloured lights dancing on a sea of expectant faces dazzled and confused her, the voice alone gave her certainty, something to hold on to. Something to desire.

'Sit down on the chair, Olympia.'

She felt the coldness of a wooden chair pressed up against the back of her legs, and sank down on to it, knees together.

'Legs apart, Olympia I want you to show me your tenderest, innermost beauty.'

Utterly unselfconscious, she let her knees slide part. Gasps and murmurs of appreciation ran around the assembled throng. Olympia was calmly displaying the secret beauties of her womanhood; moist and pink, surrounded by a fringe of abundant red-gold curls.

'Further apart, Olympia. I cannot see enough yet. I cannot see into the very heart of you.'

She strained to part her thighs.

'Good, very good. Now, Olympia. I am going to put something into your hand. I want you to pleasure yourself with it; pleasure yourself and that in turn will be my pleasure.'

He gestured to his blonde assistant, and Annick handed him a stout leather riding-crop which had stroked and bitten the flesh of many a naked beauty in the course of Laloupe's midnight shows. But already Laloupe was enjoying this woman more than he could remember enjoying any other. She was an excellent subject – so susceptible, so lascivious. He could sense her sensuality: fundamental and deep. There were no inhibitions in this golden-haired, golden-skinned beauty, and he thanked his lucky stars that intuition had led him to select her as he saw her walking into the theatre foyer. Something told him that, with Olympia Deschamps, he could act out the deepest and darkest of his many desires.

He placed the riding-crop in Olympia's hand. She seemed not to know what it was, but caressed it as though it were the living flesh of a lover.

'Here is the instrument of your pleasure, Mademoiselle Olympia. Use it wisely, use it well. Let instinct guide you; feel my hands upon you, awakening your desire.'

Olympia parted the lips of her womanhood as calmly as she would have opened the palm of a clenched fist, to reveal some treasure within. The pink pearl of her clitoris glistened, priceless and alive with desire within its fur-trimmed casket.

A slave to desire, Olympia thrust the riding-crop between her love-lips. Somewhere, out in the audience, a man groaned, overcome by the force of his need.

Lust took over swiftly, but the voice that guided her every movement refused to allow her the easy release of pleasure. Never before had Laloupe happened upon such a talented subject. He wanted this to last; he wanted Olympia Deschamps to make his show not only the talk of Paris. but the sensation of the western world.

'You are coming close to orgasm now,' whispered the voice. 'How good it feels to have your fingers on your sexual flower and a smooth hardness in the depths of you. Very, very close.'

'Yes, oh yes . . .'

Lost in the prison of her trance, Olympia began whimpering with frustrated desire. Surely a few more thrusts, a few more touches of her fingertip on her sex-bud, and she would come to orgasm? But Laloupe was relentless. He wanted to keep her sexual hunger at starvation pitch.

The clear, sweet fluid of Olympia's unselfconscious pleasure was trickling out of her now, soiling the chair on which she was sitting. Her womanhood was so well-lubricated that the riding-crop made little soft sucking noises as it slipped in and out of her.

'You may stop pleasuring yourself now,' Laloupe instructed her. And she obeyed, though every nerve-ending in her body cried out for the pleasure to continue. She sat passively, the glistening shaft of the riding-crop in her hand, awaiting the next instruction.

Laloupe paused and scanned the audience. Good, very good. He could see several men openly playing with themselves, and even one couple having sex near the back of the theatre, the woman sitting on her partner's knee as he slowly moved her up and down on his lap. Very good indeed. At this rate, he would have the whole audience indulging in a riotous orgy by the time he had finished with Mademoiselle Deschamps. He felt a sudden surge of gratitude towards this young woman, whose shameless sexuality was doing so much for his reputation.

'Olympia,' he whispered, close to her ear, 'I am going to tell you some truths about yourself now. Do you hear me?'

'I . . . hear . . . you.'

Her voice seemed incredibly distant, as though it were coming out of the ether, not from between her lips.

'Listen to me, Olympia. You are a slut. Tell me what you are.'

'A . . . slut. I am a slut.'

'Very good, Olympia. You are a cheap little slut who loves her work, and tonight you are going to be a very busy little slut. There are so many clients to be serviced, and you are so popular. Why do you think that might be?'

'I . . . don't know.'

'Then I shall tell you. Olympia, you are the most popular little slut in this city of sluts, because you will do anything – absolutely anything your clients ask of you. Do you understand?'

'I understand.'

'And are you ready to begin serving your clients? I see that there are many waiting for you.'

'I am ready.'

'You will do anything?'

'Anything.'

Inwardly, Laloupe smiled broadly. The one final hurdle was over. Now he knew for certain that Olympia Deschamps was a completely sexual creature, who would perform any act she was bidden

30

to perform. He scanned the audience again, for this stage of the show would require other people with a certain . . . talent.

Judging from the expressions of lust on the faces of the men – and some of the women too – there would be no shortage of volunteers. He hoped that those he selected turned out to have imaginative tastes.

He fixed upon a man three rows from the front, who was trying to persuade his girlfriend to go down on him. His pants were open, and he was holding the girl's hand between his thighs, but she was trying to wrest it free, red-faced and clearly embarrassed. A shame really – the fellow was quite nicely endowed, and Laloupe was sure Olympia would appreciate his stiff, thick member.

'May I have a volunteer to come up on stage?'

A few hands were raised; a few giggles erupted as friends and workmates tried to push unwilling companions out of their seats. But Laloupe was only interested in the frustrated young man in the third row. Using all his hypnotic power, he succeeded in attracting the man's attention.

The moment the young man's gaze was locked on to his, Laloupe knew he had won the battle. Much to his girlfriend's outrage and astonishment, the man got up out of his seat and began walking quickly towards the stage, not even bothering to zip himself back into his trousers.

He climbed the steps and Laloupe welcomed him like a lost son, taking the opportunity to gaze deep into the young man's eyes and make some powerful erotic suggestions to his subconscious.

'*Vous vous appelez?*'

'*Hein . . . Gaston. Gaston Picard.*'

'*Très bien. Alors*, tell me Gaston, do you excite yourself with sexual fantasies?'

'I . . . yes.'

'Tell me about them. Tell me what you would like to do with the delectable Mademoiselle Deschamps.'

Gaston hestitated for the briefest of moments, but hypnotic suggestion and frustrated lust had put paid to most of his inhibitions. With a meaningful glance at his girlfriend, he replied.

'I would like her to take me into her mouth.' The young man was trembling, but it wasn't difficult to see that he was excited. And the whole audience were behind him, calling out words of encouragement.

Laloupe turned his attentions to his prize guest.

'See, Olympia – here is your frst client. He wishes you to pleasure him with your mouth. Do exactly as he wishes. It is your greatest wish to pleasure him, for in so doing you too will feel intense pleasure. Do you understand?'

'I understand.'

Already excited by the thought of having this young man's hardness in her mouth, Olympia slid to her knees and began kissing Gaston's naked flesh. Instinct guided her hands and mouth, for she no longer had the power of conscious reasoning. She reached into Gaston's open flies and felt for his testicles; heavy and well-rounded, they tensed with pleasure as she weighed them in her palms and lavished skilful caresses on them.

Then she parted her lips and took Gaston's throbbing member between them, savouring the salty taste of the clear fluid at its engorged tip. She ran the end of her tongue over the swollen head,

32

enjoying the familiar flavour and sensation of having a man's desire in her mouth.

She sucked willingly, for Gaston's pleasure was her own now. As his testicles grew heavy with pent-up love-juice, and his shaft hardened in her mouth, Olympia felt her own excitement growing; the warmth in her belly focusing on the hard nubbin of her clitoris. And when at last Gaston gave a little shudder of surrender, Olympia wept tears of pleasure, her womanhood tensing in the first spasms of orgasm as Gaston spurted his seed deep into her mouth.

The audience applauded rapturously – all but Gaston's girlfriend, who looked on with a face like thunder.

Up on the stage, Olympia remained passively on her knees, like some eager penitent, subjected to the most curious of penances.

Laloupe's other 'guests' did not fail him. The second – an upper-crust German with a duelling scar – wanted to whip Olympia with the riding-crop. She knelt obligingly for him as he reddened her back and buttocks, convinced by the voice in her head that each new blow would bring a more exquisite pleasure.

The third demanded that Olympia straddle him, and ride him as though he were her steed; and Olympia wanted to howl for pleasure at the wild, wonderful moment of orgasm. Laloupe looked on, and was suddenly incensed with jealousy. Olympia Deschamps was his discovery, his creation. Why should others enjoy what he had nurtured? Desire burned in his belly, ate away at him like tongues of fire.

He must have her. He must . . .

'Down on your hands and knees, Olympia. Open yourself to me utterly. Would you like to feel me inside you?'

'Yes, yes. Have me.'

She was on her hands and knees now, as he had instructed. In her mind, she was a she-wolf on heat, waiting for her mate to enter her with a single thrust of his barbed member. The anticipation was becoming even more exquisite than the pleasure itself.

Laloupe unbuttoned his dress trousers with a flourish, and pulled out a handome phallus – a good seven inches long and rather thick. The audience were wild with excitement. Women wept and screamed, begging him to choose them, ravish them, do whatever he wished with them. But Laloupe only had eyes for Olympia Deschamps.

He entered her with the smooth panache of a rapier-thrust, and in her trance, Olympia felt the dog-wolf upon her, his penis hard and cruelly barbed. She twisted and turned, but the delicious agony would not go away. She did not want it to. She wanted to live within the dream forever; to go on coupling and never awake.

Laloupe rode her expertly, awakening a thousand sensations as his velvet-black voice breathed dreams into her head; he coaxed pleasure from her, and she responded as a violin to a virtuoso player.

With a sob of ecstasy, Olympia surrendered to the pleasure, thrusting out her backside to receive the tribute of Laloupe's boiling seed. As the orgasm ebbed away, she sank to the stage, panting and sweating, the trance broken at last.

She was oblivious to the audience, to the

crescendo of excitement on the seats and in the aisles, as the theatre's patrons took inspiration from the master and fell to a riot of glorious sexual expression.

Oblivious, too, to the three figures in anonymous grey raincoats who were striding purposefully towards the stage.

'Monsieur Laloupe?'

Laloupe got to his feet unsteadily, zipping his still-hard manhood back into his pants.

'*Hein, oui* . . .'

'*Sûreté. Vice Squad.*'

The man in the trilby flashed a police warrant card.

'I think we've seen quite enough of your so-called show, Monsieur Laloupe. You'd better come with us down to the Commissariat des Gendarmes.' He cast an approving leer in Olympia's direction. 'And we'll be taking the young Mademoiselle in for questioning, too.'

Olympia stared in horror at the two uniformed gendarmes who suddenly appeared, as if from nowhere, and slung a blanket round her shoulders, covering her nakedness. They were clearly not immune to her charms, and took the opportunity to run their hands all over her as they were veiling her body from public view – a little late, thought Olympia, with grim humour.

She wriggled free from their sly caresses, and turned on the elder of the two policemen.

'If you've *quite* finished groping me, Monsieur!'

The gendarme reddened visibly, and coughed.

'*Venez par ici,*' he ordered gruffly, hiding his embarrassment with a display of heavy-handed authority. '*Et vite!*'

The next thing she knew, Olympia was hand-cuffed and sitting in the back of a black Citroën with Michel Laloupe – a man who, she reflected, was not unduly disturbed by recent events. He was smiling smugly, and it occurred to Olympia that he might just possibly have engineered the whole episode. After all, notoriety hadn't done him any harm so far.

Down at the station, they were charged with public obscenity, then taken down to the cells to await questioning. As Laloupe was led away, he turned to Olympia and gave her a billion-dollar smile.

'It has been a real honour, Mademoiselle. If you should ever consider a career in professional theatre . . .'

Olympia sat in her cell, staring gloomily at the four bare walls. This was not at all what she had intended when she decided to come back to Paris. She had meant to spend an innocent evening at the theatre, and now here she was, about to be charged with obscene behaviour in a public place – and maybe even thrown in jail. She had heard some disturbing stories about French prisons. Olympia wondered idly if there was the faintest chance of seducing the Inspecteur, but discarded the thought as quickly as it had entered her head. Sex wasn't going to help her now. All it had done so far was get her arrested.

The following morning, she was taken to the courthouse to appear before the magistrate. She wondered where Michel Laloupe had got to – until she realised that he had, of course, bribed his way out of trouble. Yet again. No wonder the long arm of the law held no terrors for him. Olympia could have kicked herself for not having the foresight to think of good, old-fashioned bribery.

The magistrate was a dried-up stick of a man who made no secret of his disapproval for the young woman in the dock. Of course, Olympia had had no opportunity to go back to the hotel for any respectable clothes, and was still attired in the soiled and crumpled blouse and mini-skirt she had been wearing the night before. Last night, she had looked sensual, vampish; in the cold light of morning, she looked like a cheap tart.

She tried smiling sensuously at the magistrate, but could tell he was not amused. When he peered at her over his horn-rimmed glasses and sentenced her to five days' imprisonment, she was dismayed but hardly surprised. As she was leaving the dock, an impulse made her turn and blow a kiss at the magistrate.

His expression crumpled into a picture of perfect astonishment; then he regained his composure.

'Any more of *that*, Mademoiselle, and I'll make it a month, instead of five days.'

Olympia lay disconsolately on the scrubbed pine bench that served as a bed. So this was what prison life was like. There was certainly nothing glamorous about it. So much for her dreams of the Légion D'Amour.

She recalled the way the wardresses had eyed her as she was brought into the jail through the heavy double doors. One of them – a massive Algerian with cropped, curly hair and a Gauloise drooping from the corner of her mouth – took an obvious delight in lingering over the body search.

'*Déshabille-toi.*' The wardresss leered. '*Et vite!*'

Reluctantly, Olympia peeled off her blouse and skirt and stood shivering in her satin camiknicker, now sadly soiled and crumpled by her ordeal. She looked up at the wardress, hoping for clemency. But her gaze was returned in stony silence.

With a sigh, Olympia slid out of the camiknicker and revealed the creamy-whiteness of her breasts and the red-gold triangle between her thighs. The wardress was watching her with undisguised interest now.

'*Dépêche-toi.*' The wardress indicated a door at the end of the room, and Olympia walked through it, into a tiled bathhouse lined with shower cubicles. There were no curtains, no screens, in short, no chance of privacy. And perhaps that was the intention; Olympia's humiliation must be complete. She mused resentfully on her fate and wondered what Michel Laloupe was doing this evening.

The wardress handed her a bar of carbolic soap and a nail brush, and pushed her into one of the cubicles, turning on the water with a deft flick of her wrist. To Olympia's horror it was cold water – ice-cold. It felt like a thousand tiny, pointed needles, piercing her sensitive skin, and she tried to jump out from under the shower, but the wardress pushed her back in.

Iron hands seized her, pulling her arms behind her back so that she was immobilised and helpless. Water cascaded down her face and over the tips of her breasts.

'We have heard the stories about what you did.'

'Since you enjoy giving pleasure so much, you can make yourself useful and attend to *our* pleasure.'

'You belong to us now, *ma petite*.'

Harsh laughter surrounded her; two voices, or was it three? There seemed to be innumerable hands on her, fingers exploring her most intimate places, demanded entrance to her unwilling flesh.

She sank her teeth into the soft flesh of a hand, and an angry voice cursed her in a venomous argot of French and Arabic. The slap stung her cheek and knocked her sideways. She clutched at the wall of the shower cubicle, but could not get a grip on the slippery tiled surface, and slid slowly down, stunned by the blow.

Hands again. Prurient, insistent hands seeking out her innermost secrets. Fingers that probed her brutally, unforgivingly.

'*Qu'est-ce que se passe ici*? Stop, this instant!'

Olympia shook herself out of her daze and looked up through blurry eyes at a tall, broad-shouldered figure in the doorway.

Instantly the wardresses left her; scuttling away like startled cockcroaches at the approach of the Deputy Governor himself.

Monsieur Diavolo reached calmly into the cubicle and turned off the water. Bedraggled and exhausted, Olympia struggled to her feet and the Deputy Governor handed her a towel.

'Dry yourself, Mademoiselle. You may be a prisoner, but we are not barbarians here. I can assure you that you shall not undergo that ordeal again.'

In her gratitude, Olympia smiled up at Diavolo, and caught a gleam of covetous desire in his dark brown eyes. Well, she thought. He might be a useful ally.

They were alone in the bathhouse now, just

Olympia and Diavolo. She reached out her hand and pushed the door closed, ensuring their complete privacy. Then, very artlessly, she let go of the bathtowel, and it fell with a little swish on to the tiled floor.

'Mademoiselle. . .?'

She silenced his questioning look with a finger on his lips. Then she ran her hands over the front of his smart navy-blue trousers, smiling as she encountered the comforting swelling that marked his tumescent hardness. He tensed as she eased down his zip, but he gave a great sigh of pleasure as Olympia released his firm flesh from its prison, liberating the power of his desire.

On her knees before him, she took his penis into her mouth and showed him the power of her gratitude.

The following morning, Olympia was reading a cheap novelette when she heard the sound of a key turning, and looked up to see the cell door opening.

'*Un visiteur, Deschamps*. On your feet, and smarten yourself up!'

Olympia was amazed. A visitor? But no one – except Chris at the gallery – even knew she was in Paris, let alone prison. For a fleeting moment she wondered if Michel Laloupe had seen the error of his ways and finally seen fit to bail her out of this dreadful purgatory. But no; why should he trouble himself with a woman he'd enjoyed for a few fleeting moments – and then, only to please his fans?

Puzzled, she followed the wardress down the dingy corridor to the recreation room, where visits took place. A couple of other prisoners were at work, scrubbing the floor, and Olympia couldn't help noticing the sly looks they exchanged as she passed, nudging each other and giggling. Perhaps word of her brief liaison with Monsieur Diavolo had already spread beyond the walls of the bathhouse.

The wardress ushered her into the recreation room, then withdrew and closed the door. She would wait outside whilst Olympia talked with her visitor.

A blond young man sat at the lone table in the middle of the room. Olympia did not recognise him, but he greeted her with a welcoming smile.

'*Ah, Mademoiselle Deschamps, quel plaisir.*'

He kissed her hand.

'*Monsieur . . .?*'

'*Enchanté, ma chère.*' He sat down and indicated the second chair. 'You do not need to know me by my true name. But you may call me Valentin.'

'Why are you here? I do not know you.'

'No, Olympia, you do not know me. But I know you.' He paused. '*We* know you.'

'We?'

'The Légion d'Amour.'

Olympia felt a shiver run through her entire body – was it excitement, or fear, or both? At last, at long last, she had encountered the Légion – and here she was, doing time in a Parisian jail for offences against public morals. All in all, it wasn't a very impressive record of sexual excellence.

'I see that you are your father's true daughter,' observed Valentin. 'He was most unlucky to fail at the final ordeal. But you must understand that the Légion has its standards; standards which few

41

indeed will ever meet. But we have been watching you, Olympia Deschamps. We have been watching you and we are pleased with what we have seen.

'But, does that mean . . .?'

'Yes, Olympia Deschamps. You are ready to meet the challenge of the Légion d'Amour.'

Chapter Three

'Can't you take off the blindfold?'

Olympia clawed at the black silk scarf which bound her eyes, but hands stronger than her own pulled her fingers away, with a gentle determination.

'Patience, Olympia. When we arrive, I personally shall remove the blindfold,' promised Valentin. 'But if you refuse to sit still, I shall have to tie your hands also – and I really am most unwilling to cause you any discomfort.

'You must understand, *ma chère*, you are being taken to the very heart of the Légion; to a secret place whose very existence is known only to the most skilled and respected members of the organisation. It is a great honour. And remember: if you are to succeed in your quest, you must accept the rules and requirements of the Légion implicitly.'

Olympia gave a sign of resignation, and settled back into the softly-padded leather of the car seat. Valentin had had no difficulty in obtaining her release from prison, but she wondered now if she had been wise to volunteer herself like this for another kind of captivity. Somehow, in all the years she had longed for a chance to prove herself to the Légion, she hadn't thought it would be quite like this.

The long, black limousine purred through the streets of Paris, and Olympia sat silently between Valentin and the masked man who had met them at the prison gates. To her surprise, they did not once attempt to touch her, though she was entirely at their mercy. A vague sense of disappointment nagged at her. Somehow she had expected members of the Légion to be more adventurous, more daring, more sexual.

After what seemed like hours, the limousine swung sharply to the right, throwing Olympia againt Valentin, who clutched her tightly to prevent her falling. His hands were hot and dry on the bare flesh of her arms, and she wanted the touch to last; wanted to drink in the animal heat from his strong body so that it could drive away her fears. Then she heard the unmistakable crunch of gravel under the car wheels. This must be the driveway to a grand house, or perhaps a path through one of the public parks.

After a few minutes, the car drew to a halt and Valentin tightened his grip on Olympia's arm, helping her out of the air-conditioned car into the sultry heat of a Parisian summer afternoon. She felt gravel under her sandalled feet; then the firmer surface of a short flight of steps – stone, perhaps, or maybe concrete. At the top of the steps they paused, and she supposed that Valentin must have rung the doorbell, because a very distant jingling sound was followed by the unmistakable rhythm of footsteps coming slowly towards them along a corridor. Olympia felt a sudden hollowness in the pit of her stomach and an irritating dryness in her mouth that made her swallow hard.

The door opened with a rattle of bolts and chains.

'*Bonsoir Messieurs, Madame. Entrez. On vous attend.*'

The voice was characterless, almost to the point of being robotic, offering no hints as to the personality or appearance of its owner. Uneasy and disoriented, Olympia held on tightly to Valentin, her only landmark in a dark and featureless world.

Valentin gripped her arm and led her over the threshold, into a sudden coolness she had not expected. The air was scented with jasmine and freesia. Somewhere, in the distance, a clock chimed the quarter hour, and Olympia could just distinguish the gentle splashing of an indoor fountain. Her sandalled feet made sharp little tapping sounds on a smooth, hard floor as she took a few, faltering steps forward. She started as she heard the door click shut behind her, and a hand of fear clutched at her heart. Valentin stroked her arm reassuringly. She knew he must be able to feel her shivering, but he would perhaps put that down to the sudden chill. What would he think of her if she gave voice to her fears?

'We have arrived at last, Olympia. I trust you will forgive the discourtesy of the blindfold, but it was a necesary precaution.' He untied the silk scarf about her eyes, and she blinked in the sudden dazzle of light. 'And now the game begins.'

It took several moments for Olympia to become

accustomed to the shafts of sunlight darting in through the windows. Still rubbing her eyes, she looked around her, and saw that she was standing in the middle of a massive entrance hall. Fluted columns rose up from the polished marble floor and soared gracefully upward, towards a magnificent domed ceiling decorated with paintings of naked nympths and satyrs, bodies entwined in glorious, unselfconscious coupling.

Gazing around the hall, Olympia caught sight of two footmen in full livery, with red velvet frockcoats, buckskin breeches and powdered wigs. They turned towards her and she gave a start, for their faces were hidden by red leather masks. They looked like eighteenth-century automata – identical and grotesque.

Olympia glanced nervously at Valentin. 'So, what happens now?'

'Are you nervous?'

'Of course!'

Valentin smiled.

'It is good to be nervous.' He signed to the two footmen, who walked slowly towards them. 'These gentlemen have come to take you to meet a very important member of the Légion, Olympia. It is time now. Go with them.'

A massive, carved wooden staircase wound upwards from the central hall like the centrepiece from an old-time Hollywood set. Framed paintings and sketches lined the walls, and Olympia was amazed to see that every one she looked at was an unknown masterpiece of erotic art: exquisite Persian prints, a Leonardo cartoon, a Cézanne watercolour depicting two naked women pleasuring each other with whips and chains. Whoever lived in this house was a collector of the first rank; maybe even someone she had met many times in the world of international art dealing. She must have been under surveillance for a very long time. Just how much did the Légion d'Amour know about Miss Olympia Deschamps?

The two liveried footmen led her up the stairs and towards heavy panelled doors on the first floor landing. As they knocked and pushed the doors inwards, Olympia felt a sudden, breathtaking surge of elation. It was happening at last! After al those years, all those impossible dreams, she was at last about to enter the heart of the Légion d'Amour. Her father would have been so proud of her.

The footmen stood aside, bowing respectfully, and Olympia stepped forwards into the room. Into the deep, sepulchral darkness . . .

The doors were closing rapidly behind her, and the room was shrouded in impenetrable gloom. At first, Olympia could see virtually nothing. As her eyes grew accustomed to the darkness, she realised that she could just make out the vague shape of a four-poster bed in the centre of the room. As she strained to see more, the doors snapped shut behind her and the last vestiges of light disappeared. She was alone. Alone in a darkened room.

'Welcome, Olympia. Welcome to the house of pleasure. Tell me – do you believe you are worthy of the Légion?'

The voice sounded curiously familiar, but she could not place it. She made a last-ditch attempt to get a grip on herself, telling herself that she was no timorous little girl: she was Olympia Deschamps!

'I am worthy, Monsieur,' she replied. Then she paused. 'As was my father.'

The stranger gave a dry chuckle.

'Your loyalty does you great credit, Mademoiselle Deschamps. But you must know that your father had his chance to prove himself to the Légion. Sadly, he failed at the very last hurdle. He was a good candidate, but not, alas, quite good enough. Why should a slip of a girl like you believe that you have the ability to succeed where your father failed?'

'I have no doubt, Monsieur. I never have done.'

'I see. Then you must *show* me that you are worthy, my proud young Mademoiselle. Many have tried; almost all have failed. And never has a woman been admitted to the inner circle of the Légion d'Amour.'

'I will not fail.'

'Ah.' There was the faintest touch of amusement in the voice. 'I see you are indeed the same Olympia Deschamps who had sex with an entire rugby XV in her boyfriend's college bedsit.'

Olympia felt herself colouring with embarrassment.

'It was a tedious Sunday afternoon. There was nothing else to do. But how could you know?'

'The same proud girl who seduced her physics master because he threatened to have her expelled.'

Olympia stared into the blackness in disbelief. How could this stranger know these intimate things about her? She thought back to that day – so long ago now that it seemed like a previous life

– when Dr Atherton had threatened to have her expelled for 'immoral behaviour'.

Lymhurst College was a liberally-minded boarding school, but Dr Giles Atherton did not hold with liberalism in any shape or form. Consequently, the highly moral Head of Physics had been horrified to discover Olympia in bed one afternoon with not one, but two of the prefects from a nearby boys' public school. When he pushed open the door of the senior dormitory, one of the boys was teasing Olympia's nipples with the tip of his tongue, whilst the other was enjoying a massage so intimate that at first, Dr Atherton could hardly believe what he was seeing.

'What is the meaning of this depravity?' Atherton had thundered, slamming the door of the dormitory with such violence that the entire room seemed to shake. The two boys had leapt off the bed in alarm, trying desperately to cover their embarrassment but Olympia had merely returned Atherton's ferocious glare with a sweetly seductive smile, refusing to be intimidated by an unreasonable man who insisted on thwarting innocent, youthful pleasure. Atherton had played the wet blanket once too often.

That afternoon, Olympia had her revenge . . .

Dr Atherton had snatched up Olympia's clothes, grabbed her by the arm and dragged her, still naked, down the corridor to his office.

'I'll deal with you in there, young lady,' he had threatened grimly. 'And then we shall see what Mrs Travers-Ely has to say to this scandalous and utterly reprehensible behaviour.'

But once behind locked doors, it was not Olympia who was dealt with, but Dr Atherton.

'Get dressed immediately, Olympia. For pity's sake cover your shame. Your nakedness is an affront to common decency.' Atherton had thrust the bundle of clothes into her arms with a hard stare which was beginning to soften at the edges.

Olympia didn't get dressed. That would have spoilt the fun. On the contrary, she decided to flaunt her nakedness, and torment the old hypocrite a little. She could see he was trying desperately not to look at her body, so she stepped deliberately closer to him and pressed her un-ashamed nakedness against him. He had tried to back away, but there was nowhere to go. She had him pressed up against the wall of his own office.

'What . . . what on earth are you doing?'

There was alarm in his voice and Olympia knew her victory was assured.

'You're all excited, aren't you, Sir?'

'I . . . I don't know what you're talking about! Get your hands off me.'

'You enjoyed watching me making love with Peter and Antonio, didn't you, Sir?' She pouted seductively, and ran her fingers through Atherton's wavy grey hair. He wasn't bad-looking really. 'I wonder how long you were watching us before you decided to come into the dormitory and create a scene? Having fun, were you?'

She stretched out knowing fingers and stroked the front of Atherton's trousers, just the way her boyfriend Alex liked her to do. Panic-stricken, Atherton flinched, but the prize was hers. He was already massively hard for her, throbbing for the release that only she could give him.

'Don't be afraid, Sir. I'm just going to teach you a little lesson.'

Sliding down his zip, she thrust in an exploratory hand and was rewarded with a little sob of guilty pleasure as her fingers met the hot, hard flesh. He was big. Having him inside her would not be a chore.

He was whimpering, 'No, no, no,' but every nerve in his body was screaming 'Yes!' Olympia paid no heed to his protests, knowing exactly what he wanted. And she wanted it, too. Deprived by Atherton of her pleasure with the two boys, she was still ravenous for love.

She played with him for a little while, sliding his well-lubricated shaft gently between her fingers, then led him across the room to the shiny grand piano the music master used for his compositions. All Atherton's resistance was gone now, and he followed her like a lamb, though there was confusion in his grey eyes. She did not leave him in his confusion for long – showing him exactly what she wanted him to do. With one fluid movement of her athletic body, she jumped up on to the lid of the grand piano, and lay down.

'There's plenty of room up here for two,' she breathed, sliding her legs apart and letting her fingertips brush across the red-gold curls between her thighs. 'Don't you want me, Sir?'

'What – no, no – I can't!'

'But Sir – the whole school knows you've been giving it to Tina Brett-Fellowes since the beginning of term! Wouldn't you rather have me?'

'That's a lie – I never . . .'

Olympia rolled on to her belly and raised herself on one elbow, so that her full breasts were displayed to their utmost, tantalising advantage, her nipples pert with arousal.

51

'But Sir, Jocasta Lange saw you with her in the gym changing rooms, only last Wednesday night. What a short memory you have!' She smiled. 'But let's forget about all that, shall we? Why don't you come and make love to me, Sir? You're a very good-looking man, you know – I can't wait to have you inside me.'

The sight of Olympia – naked and shameless and crying out for him – was simply too much for the hypocritical Dr Atherton. Stripping off his shirt and pants, he climbed on top of her, his manhood pressing urgently against her belly as he bent to kiss her breasts. Olympia gave a little groan of pleasure as the tip of his hardness pressed against her love-mound, then slipped between her thighs, seeking the entrance to her tight, wet womanhood.

Atherton was an eager convert, and she was more than ready for him. She slid apart her thighs and let him enter her, delighting in his sighs and moans of lust as the warm, moist folds of her womanhood closed about him. She too, was excited; her whole body as tense and vibrant as the piano wires which sang and hummed beneath them as they began to move together, in a sweet, delicious harmony.

Oh yes, that afternoon, they really had made beautiful music together.

As the memory left her she stared into the darkness, intrigued and somehow afraid.

'Who are you? How can you possibly know so much about me?'

There was no reply, but a switch clicked on, and a small lamp illuminated the bed, casting a pool of golden light in the midst of utter blackness. On the bed sat an elderly man in a kimono of black Japanese silk. Olympia gasped.

'Do you remember me now, Olympia?'

The magistrate! Could this really be the same, dried-up old man who had glared at her so disapprovingly in the courtroom? And now here he was again, very different now, his eyes burning not with puritanical zeal but with the fires of undisguised lust.

'If you wish to undergo the trials, you must first prove your worth; prove it to me. Pleasure me, Olympia Deschamps. Pleasure me – but understand that if you fail, you shall never again enter these portals. There will be no second chance.'

'What do you wish me to do, Monsieur?'

'That I shall leave to your own imagination, *ma chère*. Seek out the keys to my pleasure. I think you will find me quite an interesting challenge.'

Olympia knew that she was equal to the test. It was one she had been preparing to meet ever since she was a dreamy schoolgirl who had just discovered the sheer physical excitement of exploring a lover's body.

She peeled off her light summer blouse and skirt, with seductive slowness. Since it had been such an oppressively hot day, underneath she was wearing nothing but a skimpy red G-string. It was fortunate indeed that she had been able to persuade Valentin to let her collect a change of clothing.

The revelation of her naked breasts evidently met with the old magistrate's approval, yet Olympia could see no sign of his desire swelling beneath the silky fabric of the kimono. She stepped out of the G-string, walked over to the bed and, bending over the magistrate, ran the fabric across his face, making sure he got the full benefit of her essential fragrance; the magical distillation of expensive French perfume and pure sex.

If she had secretly hoped the magistrate would make it easy for her by surrendering meekly to the force of his desires, she was soon to be disappointed. He allowed her to remove his kimono, then stretched out languidly on the bed, making not the slightest effort to respond to Olympia's ministrations.

Olympia gazed down at him, seeking inspiration in the body beneath her. Despite her gentle caresses, the magistrate's manhood remained resolutely limp and unresponsive.

She knelt on the bed, flesh against flesh, and sent her tongue on a voyage of exploration across his body, which was surprisingly attractive for a man of his years. His manhood refused to stiffen, and he made no sound. The legendary discipline of the Légion would permit of no weakness. It was her task to break down that discipline, and conquer with sexual skill.

Olympia tried everything in her sensual armoury to arouse the old man. She was certain he was excited by her, and yet his will was too strong for her. With the power of his mind – honed by years of sexual discipline and devotion to the ideals of the Légion – the magistrate succeeded in overcoming Olympia's most ingenious techniques.

Just as failure was staring her in the face, Olympia caught sight of the heavy twisted cord which held back the drapes on the four-poster bed. An idea came to her, and she unfastened the cord, delighting in its weight and smoothness in her hand.

At the very first stroke of her improvised lash, the magistrate's manhood began to twitch into obedient life. So, at last she had found one of the keys to unlock his pleasure. She did not hit him hard, but whipped his belly with the silken cord, and ran its tassled end between his thighs, caressing his testicles. At last he began moaning softly, and Olympia knew that victory was in sight.

'Surrender to pleasure, Monsieur. Don't fight the power of your desires.'

Swiftly she clambered astride him, her strong thighs about his hips and her eager womanhood sliding down easily over his stiffness. She rode him as though he were a favoured steed, her thighs pressing tight against his flanks. But even now he was more resilient than she had expected. She glanced down at his face, and saw the half-smile on his lips: the magistrate might be allowing himself to enjoy the experience of Olympia's body, but he was not yet ready to make the ultimate act of surrender.

The magistrate's determination to resist her simply made Olympia even more determined that she would overcome his stubbornness. Just how long could he hold out against her? There must be some little trick that would break through his defences.

She released him from her body, and the stiffened flesh slapped back against his belly, its swollen tip well-lubricated with sex-fluid. A sudden idea made Olympia pick up the silken cord once again, and she made a series of knots along its length.

This time, the beating was not a game. She brought the lash down with energy, and the knots tormented the magistrate's naked flesh like hornet stings. For the first time, he began to respond, his unwilling body twisting and turning on the bedcovers.

Again and again she brought down the lash upon the magistrate's flesh, beginning at his belly and moving inexorably downwards, towards the eager, dancing limb between his thighs. The first blow of the cord upon his balls made him cry out – the long, tortured cry of a soul in mortal agony. But there was also pleasure in his cry.

Deftly, Olympia ran a sharp-nailed finger between the magistrate's thighs, teasing the sensitive crease behind the base of his testicles; and he gave a great juddering sigh. With a smile of triumph, Olympia dug her nails deep into the flesh of his scrotum. This time, his cries were all of ecstasy.

The magistrate arched his back and then fell back upon the bed, his hot, white tribute falling in a pearly cascade around him.

Olympia bent to plant a playful kiss on his cheek.

'I told you I would not fail, Monsieur. And Olympia Deschamps *always* keeps her word.'

The magistrate opened his eyes, and hauled himself into a sitting position.

'I alone cannot pronounce your success or failure, Mademoiselle Deschamps,' he replied.

'What do you mean? You told me . . .'

The magistrate reached out to the bedside table and flicked a second switch. Instantly the room was flooded with light, illuminating the darkest corners.

'Welcome, Mademoiselle Olympia.'

Olympia gazed in mingled horror and amazement at the semicircle of masked figures seated on elaborate chairs around the edges of the room. She turned to the magistrate.

'They have been watching us whilst we . . .?'

'*Mais bien sûr*, my dear. But of course! How else are they to judge your suitability for the trials that lie ahead?'

'Well, yes, I suppose so – but who are they?'

'Oh, these are some of the most high-ranking members of the Légion d'Amour, *ma chère*. They are masked because no one who is not of the Légion may ever see their faces. They are influential men, Mademoiselle – cabinet ministers, film stars, a Nobel prize-winning scientist; men who have dedicated their lives to the Légion. Do you still aspire to join them, my dear?'

'Of course I do, Monsieur! How can you doubt it? Ever since I was a child, I have promised myself that I shall be the first woman to be admitted to the Légion d'Amour. Whatever the price, Monsieur, I am determined to achieve my goal.'

'She has spirit,' observed one of the watchers, getting up from his chair. His flies were unzipped, and Olympia saw that he had been stimulating himself whilst watching her with the magistrate. He was still erect; large and firm and tempting. 'But I must confess that I am not yet convinced she has the necessary potential to become a member of the Légion.'

'Has she the necessary stamina?' broke in his

neighbour. 'And courage? These are qualities which must be established.'

'She must also demonstrate her sexual versatility,' added another of the watchers, and he ostentatiously unzipped his flies, offering himself to her like some delicious, exotic sweetmeat.

She slid off the bed and walked confidently towards the men who had come to judge her. There was no fear now; having come this far, she was not going to fail. As she knelt and took the first man's hardness into her eager mouth, a powerful wave of arousal swept over her. There were no doubts in her mind now, none at all. Soon, Olympia Deschamps would be a fully-fledged member of the Légion d'Amour.

'You understand what is to happen to you over the coming days, Olympia?'

'I do.'

She stood with Valentin in the busy foyer of the Hôtel St Germain, her head in a whirl. She could hardly believe what had happened to her over the past few hours, and now she was back at the hotel it was tempting to believe that the whole thing had been nothing more than a waking dream. But Valentin was there, beside her and her body was still moist with the sweet, lingering perfumes of sex.

Pride warmed and elated her, making her feel deeply sensual: a creature of the purest sexuality. She had convinced every one of those cynical judges, and now it was to happen. At long last, she was to be given the chance to prove herself. She knew that this was only the beginning of her ordeal, yet she felt like celebrating. She ran lustful fingers through Valentin's wavy fair hair.

'Would you like to . . .?

Valentin smiled and shook his head.

'I really don't think you quite understand, Olympia. You must save your strength for the trials. They will be very arduous, very demanding on your sexual energies.'

Olympia laughed.

'Oh Valentin, after what I've been through today, I'm not afraid of anything the Légion can throw at me.'

Valentin patted her hand.

'You are a very brave young woman, Olympia, but please, beware of over-confidence. Do not forget your father's failure. Now, remember what I told you: there will be seven sexual trials for you to undergo over the coming days. You must succeed in all of them, for the Légion offers no second chances.'

Olympia nodded.

'How will I know when each trial is to start?'

'Each morning, at nine o'clock, a messenger will come to your hotel room. He will tell you what task you must perform that day. But now it is getting late, and I must take my leave of you. *Bon courage*, Olympia Deschamps! Perhaps, one day, we shall meet again.'

With a vague sense of regret, Olympia watched tall, blond Valentin stride across the hotel foyer, through the double doors and out into the busy street. It seemed such a pity. They could have had fun together. His warnings of dire consequences carried little weight with Olympia for as long as she could remember, she had had an insatiable appetite for sex – and she couldn't see that changing now. At any rate, she certainly didn't intend spending another night alone.

Wandering over to the reception desk, she sought out the handsomest of the clerks with a winning smile. She leant across the desk, so that he would have the full benefit of her lacy blouse, with the top button left so artfully undone.

'*Excusez-moi*,' she began. 'I wondered . . . what time do you finish your shift?'

'Eight o'clock, Mademoiselle. But . . .'

She wrote her room number on the back of a scrap of paper, and pushed it across the desk at him.

'Nine o'clock,' she whispered. 'I'll be waiting.'

Chapter Four

Olympia yawned, and stretched luxuriously in the soft double bed. It had been an entertaining, if exhausting, night and it was a pity young Arnaud had had to leave in time for the early shift. She was still in the mood for love.

She lingered under the sheets for a little while, savouring her recollections of the past night. How wonderful it had felt to have Arnaud's eager young tongue on her clitoris. He was a little inexperienced, it was true; but such an eager, gifted pupil. He had sipped her honey-dew so daintily, as though it had been some fine, rare wine. Her hand strayed absent-mindedly to her nipple. It was large and erect, tingling with the anticipation of further, perhaps even more exquisite, enjoyment. Perhaps she would just pleasure herself a little before having a shower and ringing room service for breakfast.

A loud knock on the door brought realisation crashing in on her. Oh no! The messenger! How could she have forgotten about the first of the trials?

Olympia bounded out of bed, throwing a towelling bathrobe around her, then rushed to the door and wrenched it open.

To her surprise, it was not the messenger who stood there, but the hotel manager, Monsieur Constant Faillou. He looked uncomfortable, to say the least.

'Mademoiselle Deschamps?'

'Yes.'

'I . . . this is rather awkward. Please may I come in?'

'Certainly.' Olympia stood back to let him in, then pushed the door shut behind him. 'Now, what was it you wanted to see me about?'

'I'm afraid a few of the guests on the floor below have voiced some concerns about the noise level from this room during the night. They say they have heard shouting . . . and . . . er . . . groaning.'

Of course, thought Olympia. I knew we should have tried to keep the noise down, but Arnaud was so very enthusastic. She gave Monsieur Faillou her most seductive and ingratiating smile. It really wouldn't do to get thrown out of her hotel, not on such an auspicious morning.

'I'm so sorry, Monsieur,' she breathed. 'I had a guest last night, and we got a little . . . carried away. You do understand how it is, don't you? It won't happen again.'

Already she was pressing herself up very close to the hotel manager. She could hear his breathing, staccato and shallow. Her hand brushed against his groin, apparently accidentally, but Olympia knew exactly what she was doing. The slight

62

swelling beneath the fabric pleased her, and encouraged her to go on.

She glanced at the bedside table, and was relieved to see that it was still only seven-thirty. Plenty of time for fun and frolics, after all. And she had to keep on the right side of the management, didn't she?

'I am sorry to be the bearer of bad tidings, Mademoiselle. But I simply cannot allow the other guests to be disturbed.' Faillou's voice was shaky, Olympia could tell that he was trying hard to control himself and maintain the thin veneer of professionalism that was so, so close to cracking.

'Don't mention it, Monsieur.' Olympia lowered her eyes in mock modesty. 'Really, I deserve to be punished for being so inconsiderate.' She looked up at the hapless hotel manager – who was red-faced and almost apoplectic with suppressed lust – and very calmly, began to stroke the front of his trousers. He gave a start, but made no attempt to push her hand away.

'I can't think what I can do to make it all up to you,' she breathed. 'Can you?'

He swallowed hard, and Olympia felt his manhood swelling beneath her fingertips. She squeezed the flesh, and it grew firmer still at her touch.

Suddenly, he snapped out of his sexual paralysis. The next thing she knew, his arms were round her and he was crushing her to him, kissing her passionately. His eager tongue probed the moist interior of her mouth whilst his hands explored every roundness and furrow of Olympia's delectable body.

The strength of his desire revived a reservoir of

63

half-forgotten skill within him: a boldness he had not enjoyed with any woman for a long, long time. Olympia thanked her lucky stars that nature had chosen to make her irresistible.

Faillou's hands were all over her, probing, patting, stroking, kneading. Though she had just spent a night of lust, Olympia felt completely rejuvenated, again forgetting all about the messenger who would soon be coming to set her a task for the day. Her world had contracted to this one hotel room, to this man whose hunger was burning into her like the heat from some vast inner sun.

He unfastened the knot holding Olympia's belt, and the towelling bathrobe fell open, revealing a paradise of firm, tanned flesh and releasing the scents of love which lingered still on her skin. With a groan of pleasure. Faillou fell to kissing her neck.

'Vous sentez le sexe – You smell of sex, *chérie.*

Olympia let herself melt in his arms; responding like a willing instrument to the master's touch. A new dampness between her thighs made her writhe in a long, slow dance of desire; for the throbbing at the heart of her womanhood was a terrible torment. Don't let it end, she thought, please don't let this ever end.

He was kissing her breasts now, taking one nipple into his mouth as greedily as a child sucking at its mother's bosom. His tongue flicked over the tip, making it tingle deliciously, whilst with his teeth he tormented the toughened flesh into erect wakefulness. His free hand seemed to have a natural instinct for her pleasure. In a trice it had slipped between her parted thighs and was brush-

64

ing backwards and forwards across the glossy, red-gold curls of her pubic hair.

She tried to urge him to be more assertive, more brutal, even. She wanted him to grind the side of his hand into the soft wetness between her thighs, but Monsieur Faillou's Gallic code of honour meant that he would not be persuaded to bring her too quickly to pleasure – for pleasure intensifies the longer it lasts. And he intended it to last a long time . . .

'Take me. Take me now.'

'In a little while, *chérie*. You are not ready.'

Olympia felt a tremendous warmth wash over her, and she abandoned herself to the strength of Faillou's will. She reached out and tried to caress him, undress him and hold the swelling hardness of his desire; but he would not let her. He was in control now, he would tell her what he wanted her to do – and when.

Poor Olympia was almost fainting with frustrated desire. Here she was, alone in a hotel room with a sexy young hotel manager who was gently caressing her naked flesh, stimulating her again and again to the point of no return, and depriving her of the sweet release of orgasm. The release that she needed so, so badly. She remembered how she had tormented her young lover in the lift, the previous day, and tears of frustration gathered at the corners of her eyes.

'Please, oh please; *je vous en prie*! Why are you tormenting me so?'

'The pleasure will be greater if it is a long time in coming; you know that, *ma chère*.'

He was right, of course. The longer this delicious torture went on, the more intense would be the

65

pleasure when at last it came. In her heart, Olympia knew that this was really no way for an aspiring Légionnaire to behave. Wouldn't a worthy Légion member be able to control herself and her passion, in the service of greater ultimate pleasure? She knew that she must try to be stronger; but oh, it was so very difficult when ecstasy was almost in sight.

And the ingenious Monsieur Faillou was on his knees before her now, pressing his face against her belly, breathing in the fragrance of her moist pubis as his fingertips brushed across her abundance of red-gold curls. Just when she thought the pleasure could not become any more intense, he slid his face down her belly and began running his tongue up her inner thigh as he twisted her pubic curls around his fingers, at first gently, then with greater insistence, so that the sensation was almost – but not quite – pain. The combination of delicious pleasure and mild discomfort was a powerful one, and Olympia found herself growing weak and dizzy. She grabbed at the door frame for support, but felt her fingers slipping as she slid slowly downwards.

Almost fainting with pleasure, Olympia let herself fall into Faillou's waiting arms. He gathered her up with no more difficulty than if she had been a tiny child, and carried her over to the bed, still dishevelled from the night's lovemaking. The early-morning sounds of the city floated in through the open window on a heat-haze that seemed to Olympia to carry all the million beautiful scents of sex.

She sprawled across the bedcovers where Faillou had laid her down, feeling suddenly bereft as his hands left her body and he stepped away. But he had not left her for very long.

'You are truly a beautiful woman, Mademoiselle,' breathed Faillou, swiftly stripping off his shirt and pants. 'I am a fortunate man indeed.'

Olympia was not listening. All her attentions were taken up with appreciating the hotel manager's well-honed body. His skin was a light golden bronze, smooth and sleek; and for a moment it seemed to Olympia that some beautiful, classical statue had come to life, expressly to make love to her.

Her eyes travelled down from Faillou's dark hair and grey eyes, to his broad chest, slim waist and muscular thighs. From the midst of a thick, dark thicket of dense curly hair sprang a beautiful, succulent limb of living flesh – long and slender and beautifully hard, with the most graceful upward curve Olympia had seen in a long time. Its plump head was a rich, glistening purple which begged to be licked, sucked, sampled as though it were some costly delicacy. Olympia reached out, beseeching him to make love to her, and end her torment.

'Patience, *ma chère*,' he smiled. 'First a little more preparation for you, *non*?'

He knelt down on the bed and parted Olympia's thighs, kneeling reverently between them.

This time, his lively tongue darted deep inside her, and she was not prepared for the boldness of the assault. Such a long, shameless tongue, its muscular tip wriggling eagerly into the very depths of her womanhood. In and out it darted, exciting her without ever satisfying, and she dug her fingernails into the bedcovers, stifling anguished cries as she writhed in exquisite torment.

Her clitoris throbbed with a rhythmic intensity; her entire body pulsing to the rhythm of her surging pulse. The sensations were wonderful, indescribable. Every nerve ending seemed twice as sensitive, twice as receptive as usual to this wonderful, passionate kiss. If he would only let his tongue slide across the burning bud of her passion, she knew he would bring her instantly to the heights of bliss.

Suddenly, Faillou pulled away from her, leaving her groaning with frustration. Surely he wasn't going to leave her like this?

'Why, *chéri*; why?'

Faillou bent and kissed the very tips of Olympia's nipples, and she tried to pull him on top of her. She had to have him now; had to come, or surely die of unsatisfied desire.

But Faillou grinned and shook his head, then gently prised her hands from round his waist. To Olympia's immense surprise, he rolled her deftly over on to her belly and began kissing and licking her back. Playful bunny-kisses hopped along the ridge of her spine and disappeared into the valley of her loins. Passionate kisses moistened the backs of her thighs, her legs, the hypersensitive soles of her feet. As his tongue ran down into the small of her back and across the firm hillocks of her backside, Olympia felt her entire body tense with need. Wetness was flooding out of her, staining the pale pink bedcovers. How much more of this could she bear?

Sliding his hands beneath her, Faillou pulled her up, on to her hands and knees. He amused himself for an eternity, simply toying with the magnificent curves of her backside, and squeezing her wonderful, rounded breasts. Just when she was convinced that he would never take her, Faillou took hold of her hips, and entered her in a single, powerful thrust.

In that instant, Faillou became the stallion, and Olympia his mare. Kneeling on the bed behind her, he penetrated her deeply – so deeply that he seemed to fill her entire body, each thrust pressing insistently against the neck of her womb.

'Take me, oh take me!'

'Shh,' breathed Faillou. 'The noise . . . we must be quiet.'

Olympia did her utmost to keep silent, but the effort was sheer torment. And still Faillou refused to touch the glistening pink pearl of her clitoris, to give her the one tiny gesture she needed to end the torture of her unfulfilled desire. Was this agony or bliss? She was in a hell of pleasure, a heaven of desperate need.

Faillou rode her energetically, ramming into her again and again, and Olympia thought of the little chestnut mare she had once owned, and the purebred stallion who had covered her, his huge erection distending the mare's soft flesh as he entered her. Olympia was that mare now, helpless with fear and pleasure in the face of her mate's overpowering lust. Her breath came in brief, staccato gasps as she fought to overcome the last, cruel barrier to ecstasy.

At last, Faillou's hand slipped from Olympia's hip and moved stealthily towards her pubis, toying with her pubic curls and rubbing gently on her mound of pleasure. Olympia began thrusting harder and harder, aching with lust, and begging him to touch her on that most sensitive place.

'Touch me – touch me *there*!'

And at last he paid heed to her cries, and slipped his index finger through Olympia's soft love-lips. Inside, her womanhood was a hot, wet cavern of boiling pleasure. And at its very heart, a throbbing bud of flesh.

His finger touched her clitoris.

With a cry of helpless, anguished pleasure, Olympia came to an immense orgasm that wracked her body with a series of uncontrollable spasms. Sobbing with the pleasure of release, she slumped down on to the bed. Faillou pulled out of her and rapidly brought himself to the peak of pleasure, shuddering with delight as his abundant seed showered in pearly droplets on to Olympia's delectable golden buttocks.

When Faillou had gone, Olympia dozed on the bed for a few minutes, then glanced at the bedside clock. Half-past eight! She really had better get a move on.

The shower – now behaving quite normally since the repair man's assiduous efforts – spurted into life, and Olympia threw off her bathrobe and stepped under the cool jet.

Lemon-scented shower gel revived her, and she spent a long time simply enjoying the sensation of a thousand tiny needles of cool water playing on her skin.

Drying her long, red-gold hair quickly, she wondered what she ought to wear. What *do* you wear to meet a messenger from the Légion d'Amour? What would he be like? And what task would he ask her to perform. What role would she be called upon to play today: vamp or virgin? Housewife or harlot?

She opened the wardrobe and surveyed the rail of clothes she had brought with her from London. A cocktail dress? No, surely not at nine o'clock in the morning. Jeans and a casual blouse? It hardly seemed the right ensemble for a day of reckless sexuality. Maybe the skintight black minidress with the low-cut neckline?

Paralysed with indecision, Olympia lost all track of the time. In fact, she didn't realise what time it was until she heard the knock on the door.

Too late to dress up, Olympia grabbed a big, soft bathtowel and wound it round above her breasts, tucking it in at the top. She hurried to the door and opened it.

'*Bonjour, Mademoiselle Olympia.*'

Outside stood a very ordinary man in a respectable grey suit. Surely this could not be a messenger from the Légion? He was so nondescript!

'Can I help you?'

The messenger smiled, and pushed back the longish brown hair from his forehead. He's *quite* nice-looking really, I suppose, thought Olympia grudgingly. But she could hardly believe he was any sort of virtuoso – let alone a virtuoso of sexual ingenuity and endurance.

'With respect, Mademoiselle, I think it is more a case of what I can do for you. I have a message for you.'

'From the Légion?'

The messenger put his fingers to his lips. 'Please exercise the utmost discretion, Mademoiselle. There are certain things which only the elect must

71

know. As far as the world is concerned, the Légion d'Amour does not exist.'

'Will you come in?' Olympia held open the door, but the messenger shook his head.

'I shall give you the message, and then I shall wait for you downstairs, in the brasserie next door to the hotel.' He opened his briefcase and took out a silver envelope, which he handed to Olympia. 'You may open it now.'

Olympia took the envelope from him and tore it open. Inside was a silver card, with a printed message in heavy black type.

Your task is to obtain a used sex-toy within this hotel, and present it to the messenger. You have one hour to complete the task.

Olympia read the message and almost burst out laughing. Was this the worst the Légion could devise to test her sexual prowess? If so, she was certain to pass the trials with consummate ease.

The messenger turned to go.

'I await your response with interest,' he said. 'When you are ready, you will find me in the Lion d'Or.'

Olympia placed her hand on his arm.

'No, no,' she smiled. 'There really is no need to leave. Come into my room and wait for me. This won't take long.'

This time, the messenger made no attempt to resist, and meekly followed Olympia back into the room. She clicked the door to behind him.

'Please sit down,' she instructed him. 'It's just possible you may find this entertaining.'

The messenger sank into a reproduction Louis

72

XIV fauteuil by the window, and laid his briefcase across his knees. Olympia gave a little giggle. He looked just like some pathetic civil servant, or a boring stockbroker from the Bourse. She supposed he must be employed as some sort of flunkey to the Légion. Well, perhaps this would be instructional for the young fellow.

She slid open the drawer of the bedside table, and took out a long, narrow ebony box, inlaid with silver. It was beautifully carved, and had been an eighteenth birthday present from her father.

Olympia lifted the lid of the box. There, lying on the midnight blue velvet lining, was a beautiful sixteenth-century dildo in carved and polished ivory, the plaything of some grand Tudor lady – some even said Elizabeth herself.

She discarded the bathtowel, and stood before the messenger in her awesome nakedness. He made no move; gave no sign that her magnificent body had moved him in any way – and Olympia felt just a tiny bit peeved. Well! In that case, she really would have to show this insignificant man what she could do.

Lifting one foot and resting it daintily on the seat of a chair, she bared her charms for the messenger to see, then slipped the polished head of the ivory dildo neatly between her love-lips and into the soft, wet heart of her sex.

On the few occasions when she had tried it, she had enjoyed pleasuring herself in front of a man. It had always given her an agreeable sense of power – and today was no exception. Let's face it, she thought, I'm a natural-born exhibitionist.

'Vous voyez, Monsieur, this is how I like to pleasure myself – slowly and luxuriously, with long, deep strokes. If I ever let you have me, perhaps you will remember this?'

'Assuredly, Mademoiselle.'

She watched his face, but it betrayed no sign of emotion, no hint of unbridled lust. Was this guy for real?

She made love to herself more roughly now, pinching her nipple between thumb and forefinger whilst with the other hand she worked the dildo in and out of her warm, wet tunnel. As the dildo sank deep into her, her thumb rubbed against the pink rosebud of her clitoris, already erect once more after her early-morning exertions.

'It is almost there,' she gasped, as she felt the warm waterfall of pleasure almost upon her. 'I am going to come.'

She reached the peak of pleasure: a glittering waterfall of delight which left her gasping and ready for more. But she had performed her task, and all that was now required of her was to hand the dildo over to the messenger. She could not suppress a sly smile as she slid it out of herself and presented it to him, dripping with love-juice.

'The task is complete, Monsieur,' she observed drily. 'And according to the very letter of your message. Perhaps the Légion should take greater care in the wording of its challenges.'

The messenger accepted the dildo, and placed it carefully in his briefcase. He gave a courteous bow.

'Tomorrow, Mademoiselle, at the same time. I shall not be late. Please be ready for me.'

He opened the door of Olympia's room and strode off down the corridor, looking for all the world like some earnest young businessman who had just clinched his first deal of the day.

Olympia stood in front of the mirror, thoughtfully brushing her hair. If all the challenges were going to be *that* easy . . . Well, she couldn't help wondering why her father had failed. Maybe he had just been unlucky.

A whole day in front of her, and nothing to do! Though of course, there was always work. After all, she had promised Chris that she'd do her best to hunt out some nice new pieces for the gallery, and she had made some tentative arrangements for this week with one or two galleries in Montmartre and Pigalle. Yes, that was it, she'd take advantage of the free time to do a little talent-spotting – and maybe earn herself some useful commission, into the bargain.

She searched through the wardrobe and chose a smart blouse and miniskirt, and a pair of high-heeled courts. Of course, it was much too hot for tights or stockings, and Olympia wondered if anyone would notice that she wasn't wearing any knickers.

Ten minutes later, she was walking through the foyer of the Hôtel St Germain, past the reception desk where her conquest of the previous night was sorting out a problem with one of the wealthy American guests. He tried hard not to look embarrassed as she walked past, but Olympia couldn't help noticing how his hand trembled as he tried to draw a sketch map for the tourist.

She giggled, and strode out through the plate-glass double doors into the morning sunlight, already sizzling and promising to turn Paris into a furnace at noon. She glanced at her watch: eleven o'clock. Plenty of time for coffee and a croissant before taking in a few collections in the Quartier Latin, or the Ile St Louis.

She strolled down the Boulevard St Germain, and entered the narrow streets of the Quartier Latin. Passing Algerian restaurants, redolent already with the aromas of couscous and garlic, she made her way to her favourite café.

The Café Rodolphe was teeming with life, even on this hot July day. Half a dozen different languages mingled around her, and Olympia noticed a few familiar faces from her hotel – bored hangers-on from the international symposium which was going on nearby.

She glanced around, but there seemed to be no one very interesting to pass the time with. There were a couple of rather nice Swedish men, but the way they were gazing into each other's eyes left her little hope of making any impression there. The thin, dark youth by the pinball machine looked vaguely worth cultivating, but no, he wasn't really her type – too gloomy and brooding. She took a sip from her espresso: hot, achingly-strong and with a rich bitterness that was deeply sensual. Olympia was bored. Not for the first time since she'd come to Paris, Olympia Deschamps needed a man.

The 'bohemian' quarters weren't nearly as interesting as they used to be, mused Olympia as she sipped at her coffee. Too many tourists, too many conference delegates, too many starry-eyed honeymooners – and not nearly enough real artists. Nowadays, nobody wanted to be bohemian. Starvation just didn't seem to be trendy any more. Maybe it was time to move on – take a stroll to the aa galerie, or the Galerie St Louis.

She was half out of her seat when the door of the café opned and in walked another customer.

Well, well, thought Olympia, sinking back down into her seat and instinctively smoothing back her hair. Maybe it's worth staying a little while longer, after all.

He was young, maybe nineteen or twenty at most, and as beautiful and lithe as a young animal. Silky-blond hair curled at the nape of a golden tanned neck; a hint of muscle rippled beneath the spotless white T-shirt. Tight, ripped jeans encased slender hips and strong, sinewed thighs. As he moved, she glimpsed golden flesh, flecked with bright blond hairs. A natural blond, exquisite in his youthful perfection.

To Olympia's disappointment, he did not even glance in her direction but strode directly towards the counter. She noticed that he had a large, flat parcel under his arm – a picture, perhaps?

'Ah, Joachim. *Ça va?*'

The young man shrugged his shoulders. *'Pas mal.'*

'Alors, tu veux?'

'Café crème.'

'Sept cinquante.'

The young man paid for his coffee and looked around for somewhere to sit. To Olympia's delight, the only empty chair was at her table. She arranged herself in what she hoped was a sexy posture, then picked up the morning paper and pretended to be reading it.

Joachim slid into the seat and put down his cup on the table.

'Pardon . . . le sucre?'

Olympia lowered her paper, and pushed the

sugar bowl across the table. Their hands touched momentarily as he took it, and he reddened slightly, perhaps sensing that Olympia wanted to prolong the touch.

'It is busy in here today, *non*?'

'It is always busy. Café Rodolphe is a good place to eat. And cheap! *Très* important when you are a penniless student.' He looked at Olympia over the top of his coffee cup, and she felt a frisson of lust run through her body. He had such delectable blue-grey eyes, such kissable lips.

'You're an art student, then?'

A flicker of surprise passed across those blue eyes as he lifted his coffee-cup.

'How did you guess?'

'It's not difficult. If I'm not mistaken, that's a painting you've got tucked under your arm. May I have a look at it? I know some influential people in the art business.'

'*Hein . . . oui*, I do not see why not.' He gave a wry smile and a shrug of his rather attractive shoulders. 'Mind you, I don't think you will be very impressed. Four hours I have sat there, in the Jardin de Luxembourg, and not one person has even given my picture a second look. Perhaps I really don't have any talent, after all – that's what my father's always telling me.'

He laid the picture down on the table, and began taking off the wrapping paper, with infinite care.

Of course it'll be awful, thought Olympia, wondering what mad, lustful impulse had driven her to take an interest in this gorgeous, but probably talentless, young artist. I mean, what do I do when I see it? Do I offer to buy the thing just to impress him? Or do I tell him the dreadful truth?

78

'*Et voilà.*'

Joachim pulled off the last sheet of brown paper, and turned the painting round to show Olympia.

She gasped with genuine astonishment. A riot of glowing, translucent colour shone out from the canvas – a forest of naked bodies entwined in a landscape of dreamlike perfection.

'You hate it, *non*? I knew you would. Too much imagination, too little talent, *hein*?'

Olympia laughed.

'No, no – you don't understand. It has promise. *Real* promise.'

How to tell him it was good, without telling him the truth; that it was one of the finest works by an unknown artist that she had seen in the last five years? If she gave the game away, she might have to pay him twice as much for it.

'Look, Joachim, I'll prove I like it. I'll buy it from you.'

He looked at her with real interest.

'*Combien*?'

She thought of a pittance, felt guilty and doubled it.

'A thousand francs.'

He whistled.

'*Sans blague*?'

'No kidding.' She opened her purse and laid the money on the gingham oilcloth. 'Look – do you have any other paintings.'

'Dozens. Back at my apartment. But money is short, and canvases are expensive, I was thinking of painting over some of them.'

'Good grief, no! Whatever you do, don't do that! At least, not before I've had a chance to see them.'

Olympia signalled to the waiter for the bill, paid

79

and got up from the table, towing Joachim behind her.

'But . . . where are we going, Mademoiselle?'

'To your apartment, Joachim – where else?'

Olympia followed Joachim up the last winding flight of stairs to the door of his apartment. He turned to her apologetically as he fumbled in his pocket for the key.

'So you see, Mademoiselle Olympia, some artists do still live in garrets.'

Not for long, thought Olympia. Not if your paintings all turn out to be as perfect as your wonderfully tight backside.

She followed him inside, and found herelf in a small attic studio with a sloping glass roof, letting in plenty of northerly light. On an easel in the middle of the room stood a half-finished painting of a beautiful nude; and Olympia felt a twinge of jealousy. Suddenly she wanted to be that languid blonde with the enigmatic smile, baring herself so willingly to the artist's critical eye.

Then she caught sight of the paintings stacked around the walls – twenty, thirty, forty . . .? She lost count of them all.

'There are plenty more,' volunteered Joachim. 'But they are up in the *grenier*, the attic.'

Olympia did not answer. She was too busy looking at the paintings. An exquisite landscape; portraits by the score; erotic sketches; luminous watercolours with the tints of a Mediterranean spring. She was dazzled by the wealth of talent on offer. Whatever else he might do, young Joachim was not going to escape signing up with her company. She turned to him, top button unfastened for maximum effect.

'OK, let's talk business, Joachim.'

Her hands strayed to Joachim's chest, stroking him through the thin white fabric of his T-shirt. His nipples were erect, and she kissed them tenderly as she pulled the T-shirt off over his head. The flesh of his torso was as appetising and golden as new-baked bread, with an enchanting tangle of fine, blond hairs. All the time he was looking at her, as though he could not believe what was happening to him.

She slid her hands down to his belt, hungry for his sex. The touch of her hand on the front of his jeans seemed to awaken him to reality. He was swelling under her hand.

'Business, Mademoiselle? I . . .'

She silenced him with a kiss.

'Trust me, Joachim. Believe it or not, I'm going to make you a star.'

Naked and magnificently erect, Joachim returned Olympia's passionate kiss. His arms closed about her, and the tide of pleasure carried her away as they sank together to the studio floor.

'Touch me, Joachim.'

He needed no second bidding. His hands were already on her breasts, unbuttoning her blouse, fondling and kneading her soft and yielding flesh. He unfastened the zip on her skirt, and she obligingly lifted up her bottom so that he could pull it down over her thighs.

'Toute nue! Nom d'un . . .'

Olympia laughed delightedly, glad now that she had decided against wearing any underwear. The sight of her bare thighs and glossy pubic hair was

81

enough to drive any man wild, and Joachim was no exception. He fell to kissing her all over, beginning at her lips and moving slowly and lingeringly downwards: her throat; the very tips of her breasts and the furrow between them; the soft undulations of her taut belly; the red-gold mound of her pubis, secret and sensual.

Then he parted her thighs and began lapping at her love-lips; wriggling his tongue between her labia to taste the honey-dew of her sex. She arched her back in delight as he teased and excited her, then took her revenge by wriggling away from his tormenting tongue and taking Joachim by surprise – rolling him on to his back and straddling him with her slender thighs.

'Mercy!' he cried, in mock terror.

'You shall have none!' she replied, and, with infinite slowness, she slid herself on to the tip of his erect manhood.

She felt him enter her like a hot knife sliding into butter; then, in a single, sinuous movement, he was on top of her again. She was hot, wet and ready for him; and he began riding her with long, slow, luxurious strokes. She clutched him to her, and ran her nails gently down his naked back, making him writhe and moan with pleasure.

As Olympia rose to meet Joachim's thrusts, she smiled inwardly to herself. Joachim was special. Really special. Today was turning out not to be a waste of time, after all.

Later that evening, after a pleasant dinner at the Coq d'Or in Pigalle, Olympia strolled back alone to the Métro station through the warm night air. All in all, it had been a good day. She had met

Joachim Lavallier – gorgeous, irresistible Joachim whose talent in bed was no less impressive than his talent on canvas.

In the end, of course, she hadn't been able to bring herself to do it – how can you rip off a man who's just given you six orgasms in rapid succession? She had made him a decent offer for his work, and the gallery had gained a valuable new talent. Nobody was going to lose by the arrangement. And Olympia was looking forward very much to developing a close working relationship with her new protégé.

On the corner of a backstreet near the Sacré Coeur, Olympia saw an old tramp, hunched in the shadows beside a mangy dog. Olympia normally steered well clear of down-and-outs, but she was in a good mood this evening, and more than a little the worse for drink.

She bent to pat the dog, and the tramp whispered in her ear. '*Un baiser*, M'selle; a kiss for a poor old man.'

She tried to pull away, but the tramp's hands were on her and they were strong, pulling her down until her lips were crushed up against his. His breath smelt rancid, and his clothes were imbued with the stench of cheap alcohol.

She tried wriggling out of his grasp, but he held her fast. Her heart sank as she realised that even if she succeeded in crying out, no one would pay much attention to the cries of a woman in the red light district of Paris.

His fingers probed her, enjoying every intimate fold of her body; weighing and kneading her breasts; tracing the sensuous curves of belly and backside; slipping between her thighs to explore her sexual mound.

'*Putain*! You're all wet, my darling little slut.'

Olympia tried to tear herself away, but he still held her by one wrist. Her skirt was up round her backside, and she tugged it down, desperately trying to restore her modesty.

'Don't struggle so, *belle putain*,' hissed the tramp. And there was something – a strange, glittering light in his eyes – that made Olympia stop struggling and listen to what he was saying. 'Today, you have enjoyed only pleasure and triumph. Tomorrow may be very different, Olympia Deschamps. There are six more trials for you to undergo. Perhaps they will not all be so easy . . .'

With a cry of alarm, Olympia pulled away from the tramp's grip and ran away down the alleyway, towards the relative safety of the busy Boulevard.

When she turned to look behind her, she saw that the tramp and his dog had disappeared.

Chapter Five

'*A* bientôt, Joachim.'
Olympia kissed him goodbye, then closed the door behind him. His footsteps padded softly away down the corridor, towards the lift.

Joachim Lavallier had been a more than agreeable companion to spend the night with, mused Olympia. She hoped they would be able to do it again soon. Funnily enough, she had met him on the Boulevard, directly after running away from the tramp. He'd taken her to a night-club, and thereafter events had moved so quickly that she hadn't really had to worry or even wonder about the old man's words.

As she put on her lipstick, Olympia smiled to herself, remembering what fun she and Joachim had had at the Club Zola. Of all the fetishwear clubs she'd ever been to, Club Zola was the most fun. All the 'hostesses' wore skintight leather, and the in-game was to try and guess which of them really *were* women. Most of them were rather exquisite transvestites and transsexuals – a living tribute to the art of the plastic surgeon and the corsetier.

In the centre of the Club Zola was a glass dancefloor, illuminated from below by coloured and UV lighting. At regular intervals during the evening, the dancers left the floor to make way for live sex-shows. Olympia had particularly enjoyed watching the group sex show with 'Jai' and 'Kai' – two magnificently-endowed young African guys with whom Olympia would dearly have loved to spend a little time.

But Joachim was her date for the night, and she was beginning to like him more than a little. What's more, despite his youth he had a connoisseur's taste in night-clubs, and his choice of the Club Zola had not been a disappointment.

In the shadows that encircled the brightly-lit dance floor were secluded little booths, in which guests could indulge in any sort of sexual games they fancied. In fact, so caring were the management that they even provided hosts and hostesses entirely dedicated to serving their guests' pleasure. These pretty boys and girls – dressed in leather, rubber and all manner of exotic fetish gear – went from table to table, offering their services to anyone who wanted them – for a fair price.

Olympia was delighted with this quaint custom, which she had not encountered anywhere in the world except one bar in Bangkok, where she had once spent a diverting evening enjoying an erotic massage from five hunky Chinese men.

'What would you most enjoy, Mademoiselle?' enquired a pretty young hostess. 'We cater for all tastes – oral sex, masturbation, a little domination, perhaps?'

'Oh . . . I should love to have my breasts caressed,' sighed Olympia. 'That would be so relaxing, and I'm not sure I have the energy left for anything more energetic.'

A host and hostess presented themselves: two small, dark-haired Eurasians who were clearly brother and sister. Each wore a studded leather dog-collar and all-in-one black catsuit. And both were achingly pretty.

To Joachim's surprise, Olympia chose the hostess.

'It adds a little piquancy,' she explained. 'Really, you should try it.'

And so it was that they had spent an entertaining hour in the company of a well-trained host and hostess, who had calmly and courteously pleasured Olympia and her escort, to the obvious delight of the dancers on the floor.

But no one seemed to mind in the least what guests got up to at the Club Zola – on or off the dancefloor. Olympia watched with amused interest as one girl lay down on her side on the dancefloor, and entertained not one, but five, lovers – all at once.

That night, in Olympia's hotel room, she and Joachim had relived some of the evenings's most exciting entertainments. It had been the early hours of the morning before either of them fell asleep.

Not that it mattered very much. Olympia Deschamps did not need huge amounts of sleep. But what she did need was sex – a regular supply of high-quality loving, to keep her from slipping into boredom.

She glanced at her watch, and saw that it was almost ten o'clock. Soon the messeger would be here. She knew she ought to feel nervous, after all, the old tramp had warned her not to be over-confident. But what had she to be afraid of? Olympia Deschamps could face any sexual challenge and triumph against all the odds!

All the same, the expected knock on the door brought butterflies to her stomach. Olympia put the final touches to her hair (a chic French pleat) and rearranged the neckline of her low-cut blouse. Today, the messenger was *not* going to be indifferent to her!

She opened the door. Outside stood her expected visitor, in the same grey suit and nondescript tie.

'*Bonjour, Mademoiselle Deschamps.* I trust you passed a good night. May I come in?'

Olympia led him inside, and he laid his briefcase down on the bed, clicking the clock round to the correct combination. At last he opened the lid of the case, took out another silver envelope, and handed it to Olympia.

'Today's trial, Mademoiselle. *Bon courage*, I wish you luck.'

Eagerly, Olympia tore open the envelope. Inside were a printed silver card and a 'carnet' of Metro tickets. Puzzled, Olympia gave the messenger a quizzical glance; but he remained enigmatic. She looked to the printed message for illumination.

Good morning, Olympia. Today you must travel on the Paris Métro, between Porte de la Chapelle and Mairie d'Issy.

'But . . .?'

Confused, Olympia looked at the messenger.

'Turn the card over, Mademoiselle.'

She did so, and read:

During your train journey, you must have sex with a complete stranger. Do not fail.

Olympia's head was spinning. Have sex with a stranger, on a tube train! The whole idea was ludicrous. But then again, she supposed that there might be a certain sensual pleasure to be derived from the experience.

'I will take you to the station de Métro, Mademoiselle. Then you must embark upon your quest alone.'

Olympia and the messenger got out of the car at Porte de la Chapelle. Heart in her mouth, Olympia was telling herself over and over again that it would be all right. It was well after the rush hour now; there probably wouldn't be many people on the train to see what she was up to. On the other hand, would there be anyone to have sex with?

At the bottom of the steps, the messenger left her.

'You are on your own now, Olympia.'

'But how will you know whether or not I have completed the trial?'

The messenger smiled. 'The Légion has its methods, Olympia. One day, if you are fortunate enough to be admitted as a member, you will discover secrets the world can only dream of.'

A crowd of Arabs surged along the platform at that moment, chattering and smoking hashish as

they ran through the barriers towards the train.
When the crowds had dispersed, Olympia looked
for the messenger but he was gone.

Standing alone on the platform, Olympia waited
nervously for the next train to arrive. She glanced
around at her fellow would-be passengers. Would
one of them become her conquest, her partner in
this game that had become much more than a
game to her?

The blond man, standing near the exit; he was
quite good-looking. She wouldn't mind if it turned
out to be him. Did she catch him looking at her?
An ache in Olympia's belly made her think of sex.
It would be good with him, she just knew it.

But what if she was sharing a carriage with that
horrible old man over there, coughing and spitting;
or the fat postman with the broken yellow teeth
and pendulous belly? No, no, she just couldn't!

But she knew she was in no position to start
making conditions. She must accept the task she
had been set and take her chance wherever she
found it – however unappealing the prospect
might be. And then there was the problem of
doing it without anyone noticing what she was
doing. Still, thought Olympia; where there's a will,
there's a way . . .

She remembered the time when she and her
student friend Janis had taken a trip from Kings
Cross to Cambridge, to see Clive – one of Janis's
many boyfriends – who was a medical student. He
probably did very well in his chosen career as a
gynaecologist: at any rate, you couldn't fault his
grasp of female anatomy.

The girls had been ever so slightly tipsy when
they boarded the train, that Sunday morning. This

was hardly surprising, as they had just come from an all-night party to celebrate Janis's birthday, and hadn't really had much of a chance to sleep it off. They were expecting it to be a thoroughly uneventful journey; and they certainly never anticipated what was going to happen on the 8.18 to Cambridge.

It was one of those old corridor trains that stank of mildew and Jeyes' Fluid – a creaking mass of rotting wood, overheated in summer and like a fridge the rest of the time. At that time on a Sunday morning the train was virtually empty, so Janis and Olympia had piled gratefully into an empty compartment and collapsed on to the long seats, anticipating a peaceful sooze.

They hadn't reckoned with Tom and Franco.

Just as the girls were stretching out on the seats to go to sleep, the door slid across and in came two young men, one smallish and dark, the other tall, blond and extremely hunky. They were wearing college scarves and carrying bundles of books, so it wasn't difficult to guess what they did for a living.

'Any room in here?'

'Well . . . yes; but surely there are empty compartments?'

Although intrigued and attracted by the two men, Olympia had no intention of giving up her bed lightly.

'A whole platoon of soldiers has just got on,' replied the tall blond student, apologetically. 'They've commandeered half the train.' He gave an engaging smile. 'We could sit in the corner, if you like.'

91

'Oh, let them in, Olympia,' Janis had yawned. 'I dare say they won't eat you.'

But that was just where she was wrong.

'We can take turns to sleep,' Janis had suggested stretching out on one of the seats. 'I'll take the first half-hour, then you can take over.' She had closed her eyes and wriggled luxuriously. 'Wake me up when we get to Stevenage.'

Olympia glared indignantly at the recumbent form of her friend, and had made a mental note to get her own back some time in the not-too-distant future. She, Tom and Franco had settled on the opposite seat, and Olympia took out a book.

'Ah – D. H. Lawrence!' Franco had exclaimed. 'A very great writer, don't you think? Have you read *Lady Chatterley*?'

'Of course,' replied Olympia (who had read every vaguely dirty book in English literature, and most of the French ones, too). 'But I thought it was overrated – the sex was rather boring.'

Tom's eyes had glittered with new interest.

'You're something of a connoisseur, I take it?'

'I wouldn't say that. But I believe in calling a spade a spade.'

'And an orgasm an orgasm?'

'Naturally.'

The conversation had faltered, and Olympia settled down to read *The Rainbow*. After the last frank exchange, she felt vaguely uncomfortable, as though Tom's eyes were watching her closely; but she was reluctant to look up. She remembered wishing Janis would wake up and start a conversation.

'I'm going to the buffet car,' Franco had volunteered after a while. 'Anybody want anything?'

Relieved, Olympia had dug into her pocket and brought out a handful of change.

'I'll have a coffee, please.'

'Anything for . . .?' He had nodded in the direction of Janis, who was snoring gently, catching flies with her mouth wide open.

'Oh, don't bother waking her. She's still trying to sleep off her birthday party. I'll be waking her up when we get to Stevenage anyway.'

Franco disappeared into the corridor, and slid back the door of the compartment with a click.

'Cigarette?'

Tom had offered her the packet, but she had shaken her head.

'No, thanks. I don't.'

'You don't, eh?' Tom had put the packet back into his pocket and regarded her with an ironic smile. 'So, what *do* you do, little miss perfect? Do you like to fuck?'

Olympia felt herself reddening, but she wasn't going to be thrown by a student who was hardly older than she was. She had put down her book, and stared him straight in the eye.

'I enjoy having sex. And I'm good at it, too. Probably better than you.'

If she had hoped to embarrass him, she was to be disappointed.

'Oh, I doubt it, Olympia. I'm very good.' He paused. 'Wouldn't you like to find out if I'm lying?'

At that moment, the door of the compartment slid back sharply, and Franco hurled himself inside.

'The guard!' he exclaimed. 'He's coming round, checking tickets. He'll be here any minute!'

'Oh God! I thought you said they never check tickets on the Sunday morning trains!' said Tom.

Tom turned to Olympia with a look of desperation.

'Please, Olympia – you've got to help us. If I get caught again, I'll end up in court.'

'Again?'

'Does *your* grant run to Inter-City train tickets? Franco and I could only afford one ticket between us.'

'Why should I help you?'

'Because you want to know if I was lying.'

Olympia gave a sigh of resignation.

'OK, OK, what do I have to do?'

Tom's face brightened visibly.

'Just come along with me. And bring your ticket with you. You can leave Janis where she is. She looks so peaceful.'

Tom and Olympia slipped out of the compartment and slid the door shut behind them. At the far end of the compartment was the toilet, and Olympia soon realised that this was where Tom was taking her.

'What . . .?'

'It's OK,' Tom reassured her, pushing open the door. 'It's a cinch. When the guard comes, you just shove your ticket under the door. He'll never guess there's more than one person in here.'

With severe misgivings, Olympia went into the toilet and watched Tom bolt the door behind him.

'Now, Olympia – what shall we do to pass the time?'

He reached out and pulled her towards him, crushing her mouth against his. His tongue forced its way between her lips, tasting and exploring;

and in spite of herself Olympia felt her resistance ebbing away. His hands slid over her body, appreciating is curves, its smoothness, its hollows. Her nipples were hard, and he could hardly fail to notice them as his hand slid up underneath her cashmere sweater.

He unfastened her bra, and lifted it up at the front, exposing her breasts.

'I want you, Olympia. And I'm going to have you.'

His lips had strayed from hers, and laid a trail of kisses from neck to breast; fastening on her right nipple whilst his fingers teased and tormented the left. He didn't lie, Olympia had thought. He really is pretty good. But I'm even better.

There wasn't much room to manoeuvre in the cramped compartment, but Olympia was determined. As Tom sucked at her nipples, she reached down and unzipped his flies. Even before she touched the flesh within, she knew that it was beautiful and deliciously hard. She began kneading it, very gently and very slowly, as with her other hand she teased the downy blond hair that covered his heavy scrotum.

He responded to her touch, groaning with pleasure as she delighted him with her expert caresses; and Olympia knew that, unless she was very careful, he would come before she had had a chance really to enjoy him properly.

Tom, too, was hungry for more adventurous sex. His hand was under her skirt, delighting in the naked flesh between stocking-top and black lace panties; wriggling his fingers inside the gusset, to taste the divine wetness of Olympia's secret mound.

95

'You're ready for me, Olympia,' he breathed. 'You can't hide your desire from me.'

Olympia answered by rubbing his penis harder, so that he gave a little sob of agonised pleasure. Her pleasure was in his hands, but he had surrendered first.

To Olympia's alarm, Tom had reached into his pocket and took out a penknife, which he flicked open with consummate ease.

'Don't worry, sweetheart. I'm not going to hurt you.'

Lifting up her skirt, he inserted the point of the penknife under the elastic of Olympia's lace panties, and slashed the left side open. He repeated the exercise with the right side, then pulled off the panties, rolled them up and shoved them in his pocket.

'You have a delicious backside, Olympia. Would you like me to have you now? Or is that something else you "don't do"?'

'There's no room in here to do anything,' retorted Olympia. 'And the ticket collector will be here in a minute!'

Tom laughed. 'Just watch,' he replied. 'I'll show you what we can do.'

He let go of her and bent to put down the lid of the lavatory seat. Then he lowered himself down on to it, his erection arching upwards out of his open flies. It was hard, plump-headed, glistening with delicious moisture.

'Turn your back to me, Olympia,' he had instructed her. 'Now lower yourself on to me – I'll guide myself into you.'

She had obeyed, not out of subservience but out of need: she had been hungry to have a man inside

96

her again. The party had been such a disappointment: all night long she'd danced with a series of young, available, good-looking men, and not one of them had given her what she wanted – exciting, adventurous, intensely satisfying sex.

He slid into her smoothly, steadily; thwarting her desire to swallow him up in a single, desperate thrust. He knew that the excitement would be so much greater for them both if they took this slowly.

'Aah,' sighed Tom as she sank the final inch on to his upthrust manhood, and its tip pressed against the neck of her womb.

'Quiet,' hissed Olympia, though she scarcely knew how to keep from crying out herself. 'Someone may hear us.'

As though reading her thoughts, at that very moment someone had rattled the door handle. Voices filtered through from the other side – a woman and child wanting to use the toilet.

'Tell them you're ill,' whispered Tom, all the time working Olympia slowly up and down on his prick.

'I'll . . . be – as quick as I can,' gasped Olympia, not entirely dishonestly. 'I'm . . . not feeling very well.'

'Sorry to bother you, love. I'll try the one in the next carriage.'

They breathed a sigh of relief.

Olympia was almost weeping with pleasure, and she could feel the desire in Tom rippling through her. His hands were on her thighs, and as she looked down she saw that his knuckles were white with the effort of keeping silent.

Taking control then, she seized the rim of the

cracked yellow washbasin, and used it to lever herself up and down more strongly on her lover's lap. With each downward stroke she reached back, between her legs, and let her fingertips brush Tom's balls, teasing him with her butterfly touch.

'Do it to me, do it to me,' he had moaned. And Olympia felt his surrender was very near. A few more strokes only, and he would spurt into her. She must delay him until she, too, was at the moment of crisis. She took her hand from his scrotum and started playing with herself. Looking up into the mirror, she saw the scene and it was engraved forever on her memory: a young girl, her breasts and thighs bare and her red-gold hair tumbling over her naked shoulders, sliding down onto the erect penis of a blond youth whose mouth was open in a silent cry of ecstasy and abandonment.

Knock. Knock.

'Tickets, please!'

Orgasm was so near now that neither Olympia nor her *amant de passage* could halt its inexorable progress.

'The ticket,' gasped Tom in her ear. 'Under the door.'

With all that remained of her strength, Olympia pushed the ticket into the gap beneath the door, and it disappeared. At the same time, pleasure caught up and overran her, shaking her body like a doll in a lion's mouth.

Tom was twitching inside her, and she knew he was coming too, his hot, white seed jetting into her in a series of abundant spurts. His fingernails were digging into her thighs so hard that they caused her pain; but all Olympia could think of was pleasure, pleasure, pleasure.

The spasms had overwhelmed her, and she sank back on to the lap of the helpless Tom, who was trembling in the last throes of orgasm.

There was a sharp click, and the ticket reappeared under the toilet door.

'Much obliged. Sorry to bother you.'

When Tom and Olympia finally got back to their compartment, they were almost at Stevenage and Janis was snogging with Franco. The two of them sprang apart guiltily as the door slid open.

'Don't let us interrupt you,' Olympia had said, acidly. 'Had a nice sleep?'

When the train finally drew in at Cambridge, as they all alighted, Olympia watched the two lads hauling their bundles of second-hand books out on to the platform. It seemed a shame, really, that they would never meet again.

Unusually, the ticket barrier was manned and a porter stuck out his arm as Tom and Franco went past.

'All tickets.'

To Olympia's amazement, Tom reached into his pocket and took out a second-class return, which he handed to the porter with a polite smile.

'But . . . but you had a ticket all along!' exclaimed Olympia, confused and indignant.

Tom grinned broadly. 'Yes, I did, didn't I?'

'Then why . . .?'

'My dear – how else could I have got you to have sex with me on the 8.18 from Paddington?' He reached into his pocket again, and took out a couple of triangles of lace-trimmed silk, still fragrant with the unmistakable odours of sex. 'Yours, I believe.'

As she stood and stared after him, open-mouthed, he turned back and gave her a cheery wave.

'See you around!'

Not if I see you first, thought Olympia.

Janis never suspected a thing.

That day seemed so long ago now; yet it was only a matter of five or six years. Olympia had grown up a lot since then. She couldn't count the number of times she'd wished she could meet up with Tom again, and have her revenge. Now, standing on the platform at Porte de la Chapelle, it was all coming back to her. The blond young man looked so like Tom – tall, thick-set, with an arrogant set of the jaw. Having him would be like taking her revenge on the smooth-talking bastard who'd tricked her, all those years ago. Already she was planning how to do it.

As the train drew into the station, Olympia collected her thoughts and reminded herself that this was her only chance: she must not fail.

To her dismay, the carriage was a lot fuller than she had expected. Mothers, children, businessmen and women; and even – to her utter horror – a couple of gendarmes! This was madness, it was just not going to work.

They rolled out of the station, picking up speed; and as the train rounded a bend into the blackness of the tunnel, Olympia set about selecting her 'victim'. There weren't many to choose from. A couple of elderly men with a poodle; a spotty young man who might perhaps have aspired to a job as a bank clerk if his ears hadn't stuck out so much; and a middle-aged businessman engrossed in an amateur photographic magazine.

She selected the middle-aged businessman as the best of a bad bunch, edging nearer to him until she was standing right in front of him. Now, how was she going to attract his attention? Luckily, he was sitting right in the corner of the carriage. If she kept her back turned to the rest of the carriage, maybe they wouldn't see her unbuttoning her blouse, showing him her breasts.

The train went round another bend, and Olympia took advanage of the slight lurch to rub her leg 'accidentally' against his. At last the businessman looked up. A look of immense surprise passed across his face as he saw Olympia's gaping blouse, her naked breasts beneath, and her lewd fingers massaging them.

She must work fast. Already the train was pulling in to the first station.

'*Vous voulez, Monsieur?* We could go into the guard's compartment and have a little fun.'

The businessman laughed.

'*Pardon, Mademoiselle.* But you are . . . not quite my type. *Allons, Bernard.*' He turned to the spotty youth and they both got up from their seats. Olympia watched despondently as they got off the train.

At the first station, a huge crowd of Japanese tourists got on to the train, and Olympia groaned inwardly as she was crushed up against the door into the next carriage. In desperation, she wrenched it open and escaped into the next compartment, slamming the door behind her.

This carriage was not much better. But Olympia was immediately drawn to a tall, dark man sitting at the other end of the compartment. He was certainly not classically handsome, but his aquiline features were stylish, elegant. His clothes were expensive and well-cut, and he wore his black, wavy hair in a longish, almost Gothic style. He was wearing dark glasses and appeared to be staring into space, deep in thought.

As she got nearer to him, he seemed to sense her approach and looked towards her. She cursed the mirror shades that hid his eyes from her, refusing to betray any expression.

No one paid much attention to Olympia as she made her way down the carriage until she was standing in front of the man. She opened her mouth to speak, but he got in first. 'You smell of violets, Mademoiselle. Sweet, summer violets and sex.'

His voice was smooth and resonant, and it sent little shivers down Olympia's spine.

She bent down and kissed him, and he seemed both surprised and pleased. His hands skimmed the front of her blouse, no doubt noting the naked breasts bobbing unfettered beneath the flimsy fabric; and her hard, yearning nipples.

'I want you, Monsieur.'

He gave a little gasp as she ran her hand up the inside of his thigh, briefly touching his balls and verifying that he was indeed in a state of some excitement. But he made no attempt to make a grab for her, or unbutton her blouse.

'Do you not find me attractive, Monsieur?'

He laughed. A strangely dry, ironic laugh. Then he pulled her face down to his and kissed her.

'I cannot say that, Mademoiselle. Though assuredly you smell and feel and taste divine.'

'I don't understand. What . . .?'

He made no reply, which irritated Olympia. Desperate situations called for desperate remedies. She would show him; and the rest of the passengers too, for that matter.

She hauled her victim to his feet, and pushed him up against the end wall of the carriage. He was breathing hard, and she knew he wanted her. All eyes were on them now, but she didn't give a damn. There were only a few stops to go, and if she did not have sex with someone before she got to Mairie d'Issy, her dreams of joining the Légion would be shattered forever. Besides, this enigmatic man intrigued her. He posed a challenge she simply could not resist.

Olympia unzipped his flies with a quick, efficient movement. He relaxed in her hands and seemed happy to surrender to her will, though the same semi-ironic smile still played about the corners of his mouth.

He was erect and ready for her. She bent to kiss and lick his flesh, and it tasted wonderful. She lapped up the clear sex-fluid that adorned the tip of his penis, and with each lick another glassy tear would appear at the little, weeping eye.

'*Pour l'amour de Dieu* . . .'

He was moaning now, and clutching at her hair as she went down on him. As his pleasure increased, so did Olympia's lust, and she felt a familiar, moist glow spreading through her loins. This was fun, but it would be a great deal more fun to have him inside her.

There was a sudden, expectant silence in the carriage. Olympia did not turn round, but she knew that eyes were boring into the back of her head, willing her to the final act of defiance in front of all these witnesses.

She lifted her right leg and her lover supported her with his hand under the knee as she lowered herself on to his willing hardness. As he slipped into her, he threw back his head and gave a long, low growl of satisfaction.

'Velvet,' he breathed, 'Sweet, soft velvet.'

Olympia knew that her audacity must now leave nothing to the other passengers' imagination. Her skirt was up round her waist, exposing her bare, creamy buttocks and the red-gold fringe of her pubic curls. The thought that a dozen people, maybe more, were watching her taking her pleasure, excited Olympia; and she rode her lover with skilful eagerness, caring nothing for what her fellow-passengers might see, or think.

They moved together beautifully, with a natural synchronicity which was so rare in a transient lover. His arms were strong, his hands under her backside, moving her up and down on his hardness as easily as if she weighed no more than a feather. She so wanted to make it last, but the train was speeding on through the tunnel, and in a few minutes they would be at the terminus.

Torn between desire and ambition, Olympia forced herself to accelerate the pace of their love-making. An irresistible warmth was in her belly, making her tremble with the anticipation of ecstasy.

His hands were clutching at her, his fingernails digging into the soft flesh of her bare buttocks. Got to come; got to come now . . .

She became aware of a sound all around her, like a low hum; and with a start she realised that the other passengers in the carriage were murmuring softly to themselves: 'Come, come, come.' Their voices teased and excited her, and she felt the man's pleasure spurting into the very depths of her as he gave up his tribute with a long, luxurious sigh.

Desire exploded in her like a starburst of many-coloured lights, and she clutched at her lover as he bent to kiss her passionately upon the lips.

'You taste of honey, my darling. And your scents are all of the sweetness of sex.'

Together they entered the spinning maelstrom of pleasure, emerging on the other side, exhausted but happy.

Pulling her skirt down over her backside, Olympia eased herself off her lover's still-erect manhood and turned to confront the other passengers in the carriage. To her surprise there was no sign of their previous excitement, their sense of involvement in what had happened only feet away from them. They were all looking away – some apparently engrossed in newspapers, others in animated conversation, or simply staring silently into space. It was as though nothing had ever happened.

The train was nearing Mairie d'Issy. Time to tidy herself up and get ready. She turned back to the man who had so willingly offered her a passport to success.

'Thank you,' she said, planting a kiss upon his cheek.

'The pleasure was all mine, Mademoiselle, believe me.' The man smiled, and stroked the contours of her face. 'It is not often that a blind man has such enchanting company.'

Olympia gaped in astonishment; lost for words.

To think she had been so crass, so unobservant! She wanted to say something, to apologise to him – though she didn't know what for – but the station was rushing towards them, a dazzle of white light and faces, huddled together on the platform.

The train drew to a halt, and the doors slid open. Caught in the rush of passengers, Olympia found herself on the platform before she realised what she was doing. As the train slid out of the station, she saw her transitory lover sitting in the same seat, hands neatly folded in his lap and a secret smile on his thin lips.

'A passable performance, Mademoiselle; executed with some ingenuity and resourcefulness. Allow me to offer my sincere congratulations.'

Olympia wheeled round to see a familiar, characterless figure standing on the platform behind her. It was the messenger, wearing the same anonymous grey suit but this time carrying a clipboard and pencil. He looked more than ever like some pettifogging minor civil servant as he placed a tick against the words *'Deuxième épreuve'*.

'So I passed, then?'

The messenger gave a polite little bow.

'I confess I was not sanguine about your chances of success, Mademoiselle Olympia. It takes courage to proposition a total stranger on a Métro train. You have done well. But of course,' he smiled, 'this was one of the easy trials. Your journey has hardly begun.'

Chapter Six

*T*hat night, Olympia enjoyed a long, romantic dinner with Joachim at the Café Rouge, where they discussed his forthcoming London exhibition, which Chris had provisionally entitled 'The Sensual Landscape'. Joachim had work he needed to finish back at his studio, so she went on alone to a seedy backstreet cinema in the red-light district, to watch a couple of skinflicks and savour the lowlife all around her.

It was late when she got back to the hotel, so she just kicked off her shoes and flopped down on the bed, too tired to get undressed. As she reached out her hand for the bedside light-switch, her hand encountered something else; the worn binding of a small leather-bound book, the pages held shut by a small lockable clasp.

Her father's diary.

Olympia picked up the battered little book, and wriggled up to the bedhead until her back was leaning comfortably against the wall. Cross-legged on the bedspread, she unlocked the clasp and opened the diary at random. Although she had read the words many times before, they never failed to inspire her.

Saturday, June 5th. Tonight, the messenger came to me and gave me an envelope with details of my next trial. I was to go to the French cinema on the outskirts of Algiers, and have sex with the first woman who offered herself to me.

I arrived at the cinema around seven-thirty. A greasy-haired woman in a tight black frock sold me my ticket, and I hoped earnestly that she would not volunteer to be my first conquest. Fortunately, she did not offer me her body, though she leered at me suggestively as she handed me the ticket and told me: 'We are always glad to welcome such a distinguished gentleman. I'm sure you're going to have an *enjoyable* evening, Monsieur.'

The inside of the cinema was dingy, to say the least, and the stiflingly hot air was permeated with an indefinable yet overpowering smell, a nauseating blend of a thousand rank odours: cheap wine, garlic, hashish and stale sweat. I suppose the owners of the cinema saw little point in giving it a good clean or a fresh coat of paint. After all, the patrons were not there to admire the decor.

It was an old-fashioned picture house, with seats more like armchairs than the familiar tip-up bucket seats, and a good distance between the rows. Oh well, I thought to myself, it might be a flea-pit but at least I would have plenty of space to stretch my legs.

A devilishly pretty Arab boy with long, silky eyelashes showed me to my seat, and I felt his delicate, girlish hand brush across my thigh as I eased my way past him to sit down. His offer tempted me momentarily, but mindful of the messenger's instructions, I shook my head. I must keep my wits about me tonight, with so much at stake. 'Later, perhaps,' I told him, and he disappeared back into the darkness.

A dull ache of apprehension throbbed in the pit of my stomach. To tell the truth, I found it difficult to imagine anything in the least sensual or erotic happening to me in this sad, almost forgotten place, and yet I knew that the Légion must have planned the scenario down to the last detail. I glanced around me in the semi-darkness, and made out the still, silent shapes of perhaps a half-dozen patrons, none of whom paid me the slightest attention, as they were all clearly transfixed by what was happening on the screen.

The film had already begun, but it was not difficult to catch up on the plot – if indeed you could call it a plot. On the screen, an unlikely-looking nun was lifting up her skirts to accommodate two lascivious monks, one thrusting deep into her whilst her lips worked greedily between the other's thighs. She was no great beauty, but those brazen scarlet lips encircled her lover's flesh most alluringly. Her two suitors were quite handsomely endowed, and in spite of my reservations, I soon found myself beginning to become interested in the tawdry spectacle.

I darted furtive glances along the row of seats,

and was relieved to see that there seemed to be no one with a clear view of what I was doing. By now, I had such a massive erection that it was almost painful. So, unbuttoning my trousers there and then, I eased out the stiff flesh and began to play with myself.

So carried away was I with my solitary pleasure that I did not at first notice the tall, striking brunette who was making her way down the side aisle towards me. In fact, I didn't notice her at all until she slid elegantly into the seat next to mine.

'Mind if I sit here, honey?'

The soft, San Francisco accent made me tingle with anticipation. This woman was not at all like the strident, brassy young strumpet on the screen; her voice was low, husky, with wonderfully warm and sensual overtones that made my whole body vibrate to the rhythms of lust. She had real class. My heart leapt: if this exotic Venus was to be my first conquest, my visit to the Théâtre Alhambra would not be so great a trial, after all!

The woman was tall and well-formed; her swelling breasts firm and stately under her strapless, sequinned evening gown. The scarlet fabric of the dress clung to her perfect figure like a lover's embrace, setting off the warm hazel of her skin and the glossy black hair that fell in ringlets over her tanned shoulders. A true flower of the desert.

'I . . . no, of course not. Please do.'

She must have seen me playing with myself, but she betrayed no sign that she had noticed anything amiss. I watched her out of the corner

110

of my eye. She was pretending to be engrossed in the film, but her little charade didn't deceive me. Her nipples were large and stiff, pressing against the fabric of her dress. The cinema seats were roomy and yet she was sitting very close, her flesh felt hot and firm through the fabric of my shirt and pants as she pressed against me. I wanted her so much, and cursed both my gentlemanly reserve and the Légion's strict instructions. If I was to have this woman, she must offer herself to me.

I need not have worried. My glossy-haired temptress had the seduction scene well in hand.

'Kinda hot in here, hon, don't you think? What d'you say we get a little more comfortable?'

I turned and saw that she had slipped down the shoulder-straps of her gown, and I watched spellbound as the sequinned fabric of the bodice peeled slowly downwards, gradually revealing more and more of her glorious breasts. Then I gave a little start as I felt the woman's hand on me, unbuttoning my shirt and running strong, skilful fingers over my chest.

Emboldened, I slid my hand across and touched her thigh through the split-sided gown; the delicious warmth of her taut, silky-smooth flesh seemed to burn into my palm as I stroked and caressed.

Crazy now with desire for her, I tried advancing my hand further up her thigh, until I was almost touching her pubis. I longed to bury my fingers in her wetness. But, to my intense disappointment, she blocked my hand and lifted it gently from her thigh. As I looked on questioningly, she reached across and placed her hand in my lap, stroking the throbbing manifestation of my desire. I must have let out an involuntary groan of hunger, for she smiled and placed a finger to her lips.

I sank back into my seat as she took control of my pleasure. Excited as I already was, she had not the slightest difficulty in bringing me close to the point of no return; but just as I reached the critical, unbearable moment, she stopped masturbating me. Her fingers still lay curled about my engorged flesh, but she made no attempt to go on stimulating me, and when I looked into her face I saw a wicked smile playing about her moist red lips.

I could hardly believe that my seductress could be so cruel, and – in an agony of frustration – I tore her hand from me. Her smile did not even flicker as I ripped down the front of her strapless gown in a single, frenzied movement.

On the flickering screen, a semi-naked novice with luscious, womanly curves was performing fellatio on a middle-aged man in a Bishop's cope and mitre. Bu the actress's breasts, magnificent though they undoubtedly were, could not in any way compare with the firm, bare flesh I now kissed and caressed with a diabolical fervour.

Never have I tasted a woman's flesh like it; this woman's nipples were salty-sweet, like the kernels of some exotic fruit, dried to a leathery toughness in the tropical sunshine. I lapped and nibbled and stroked and petted, and my temptress seemed pleased with my ministrations, for she laughed and threw back her head, her glossy raven locks streaming over the soiled maroon moquette.

I wanted her so much; and I recalled what the messenger had told me. This woman had offered herself to me, in the darkness of the cinema; and I must have her if I was to find favour with the Légion – though I must confess, I was driven now far less by duty than desire. The taste of her exquisite breasts had served only to sharpen my appetite for her delicious flesh.

She must have read my thoughts, for just as I was about to place my hand upon her thigh once again, the woman turned her face to me and spoke. Her soft, smoky drawl made me mad with lust for her.

'I want you, goddamit. I want to have you now: this minute.'

She stood up, and I wondered where she was going. Perhaps she was going to lead me out of the auditorium into some seedy dressing-room; or out of the cinema altogether, and into a stinking back-alley where the most profane delights might pass unnoticed?

To my surprise, she simply bent forward over the empty seat in front, and began hitching up the skirts of her sequinned gown. Underneath, she was wearing a pair of black satin French knickers.

I smoothed the flat of my hand over her thighs, up underneath the hem of her knickers, and then tried sliding a finger into the moist cleft between her thighs; but she shook her head.

'I want you to take me from behind,' she commanded me, her soft drawl taking on a note

113

of authority. 'Pull the gusset of my knickers to one side, and slide into me. I will guide you in.'

I did as she told me, and in a single thrust I was inside her. She was hot, hot as a volcano, and it felt as though a fiery hand was masturbating me, with demonic skill. I slid my hands round her hips, but she would not let me play with her, preferring to stimulate herself by rubbing her hand over the front of her pubis. Instead, I toyed with her breasts, letting their glorious bounty overflow my greedy hands.

At last, I felt her shudder beneath me and knew she was coming. With a few final strokes I joined her in ecstasy, and as I spurted into her I looked up at the screen, where a naked girl was arching her back in helpless, silent pleasure.

When I pulled out, the woman remained motionless for a few moments, slumped over the seat, gasping to get her breath back. Finally she drew herself up and, pulling her dress down over her backside, turned round to face me with a satisfied smile.

But she did not pull her skirts down quite quickly enough; for, as she turned I glimpsed the diverting truth of my adventure: the outline of a man's penis, lively and still erect.'

Olympia chuckled to herself as she read her father's account of his encounter with Rosalie, the exquisite transsexual who knew a thousand ways of pleasuring a man with her mouth – and a thousand more of bringing him to orgasm with her delicious backside. Even now, years later, Olympia admired her father's spirit of adventure. It was a tragedy that he should have failed in his endeavours to join the Légion. An even greater tragedy that he should have died without ever seeing his daughter, following so valiantly in his footsteps.

There could be no room for doubt in Olympia's mind. She was going to set the course of history straight, once and for all. She owed that much to her father – and herself.

'I can assure you, Mademoiselle; there is no mistake.'

Olympia stared again at the card, and then back at the messenger.

'You want me to . . .?'

'Indeed, Olympia. Your task is to seduce seven virgins before dawn tomorrow. That is perfectly clear, is it not?'

'Yes, of course, but *seven*?'

'Seven. The Légion is quite specific on that point, I think.'

'I'm not sure there *are* seven virgins in the whole of Paris!' exclaimed Olympia, not sure whether to laugh or cry.

'If you cannot perform the task, Mademoiselle Olympia, you have only to say. If there is some problem . . .'

Olympia drew herself proudly up to her full height and threw the card on to the table, in a dramatic gesture.

'There is no problem, I assure you. I give you my word. And when Olympia Deschamps gives her word, she always keeps it!'

Olympia sat on a bench in the Jardin de Luxembourg, and contemplated the endless procession of passers-by in gloomy silence. It was two o'clock already, and she hadn't tracked down a single virgin yet, let alone one eager to be seduced. She had been to all the tourist traps – the Centre Pompidou, the Eiffel Tower, the Bois de Boulogne – and a series of depressing *auberges de jeunesse*: in short, everywhere she could think of where she knew she would find young people. She'd had several interesting offers – but as yet, no virgins!

Time was running out.

In the distance, a group of nannies and upper-crust mothers were sitting chatting whilst their pampered charges ran around chasing the pigeons. Olympia was beginning to think that the only place she was going to find seven virgins was in a kindergarten.

Then two priests strolled past deep in conversation, bat-like in their flowing black soutanes. At that moment, the germ of an idea formed in Olympia's head. The Lycée St Siméon! The most exclusive boys' private school in all of Paris. Everyone knew that place was run like a prison – it would be bound to be packed with willing young virgins! But it was run by an enclosed order of monks. How on earth was Olympia Deschamps ever going to get in?

And yet, hadn't her cousin Monique once taught music in a Jesuit boys' school?

Getting up from the bench and smoothing down her skirt, Olympia walked swiftly towards the main gate. She had some important telephone calls to make.

At eight o'clock that evening, Olympia found herself standing outside the Lycée St Siméon, briefcase in hand. As she gazed up at the massive black

116

oak door, she could hardly believe that she had talked her way into a job in this gruesome place. You could hardly call it warm and welcoming, more like Dracula's castle in a low-budget horror movie.

She was feeling more than a little apprehensive. This must be the craziest thing she'd ever done. Surely she would never get away with it. For the first time, she thought seriously about chickening out, just turning around and walking away from the school, the trial, the Légion. Then she remembered her father's diary, and all her hopes and dreams came flooding back. No, she told herself; maybe in the end I'm going to fail, but I'm giving this my best shot.

Her assumed identity – that of a visiting piano teacher – was the best she could manage at such short notice. She thanked her lucky stars that Mr Peterson had been so strict about her piano practice, and, rather shakily, she walked up to the front door of the school.

A bell jangled somewhere in the distnce, and after a little while a rusty metal grille slid open. An elderly face peered out at her, quizzical and slightly disapproving.

'Bonsoir. Je m'appelle Mademoiselle Deschamps. The temporary piano teacher. I believe the agency rang you, earlier this afternoon . . .?'

'Ah, yes. Well, as I am sure you appreciate, Father Abbot does not generally admit women teachers to the school, but the agency spoke most highly of you. You may enter.'

He heaved open the old oak door, and she stepped inside. The elderly brother looked her up and down with a critical eye, and she was glad she had decided on the sober grey suit.

'Such a pity that Monsieur Ducard was taken ill at such short notice,' remarked the brother. 'But needs must, and the boys do look forward to their daily piano lessons. I understand you will be having some of our most gifted pupils this evening.'

I do hope so, thought Olympia. Seven will do.

The elderly monk led the way. The Lycée St Siméon had the universal smell of all boarding schools – a mixture of pine-scented disinfectant and boiled cabbage – and Olympia felt suddenly more at home. They walked together in silence down a long, dark corridor, past the Principal's office and up several interminable flights of stairs which took them, at last, through a maze of corridors to a door marked 'Music Room'.

'All the piano lessons take place in here, Mademoiselle. Please do not hesitate to exercise the strictest moral discipline. As I am sure you will appreciate, our pupils lead an extremely sheltered life, and do not often share the society of women. That, I might add, is exactly as their parents wish it to be! Kindly leave the keys in Father Abbot's office on your way out of the building.'

The elderly brother left her, and Olympia pushed open the door. The sight that greeted her was not quite what she had expected. Instead of a group of hunky fifth-formers, Olympia was confronted by three of the freshest-faced young boys she had ever seen – dark-haired twins, and a blond boy with the angelic features of a cathedral chorister. None of them could have been any older than eleven. Olympia's heart sank. She might be desperate, but even she would not stoop to cradle-snatching.

Her first instinct was to apologise, turn round and march straght out of the school. But it was too late. One of the dark-haired boys was already bounding forward like a puppy. She groaned inwardly as he seized her by the hands, dragging her towards the piano.

'Oh, Mademoiselle! It is so good to meet you! I am César, and this is Gilbert and my brother, Anton. Will you play for us, please? And will you listen to our nocturnes? We have been practising so hard all week.'

With a sigh, Olympia sat down on the piano stool and opened her music case. This was going to be a very, very long evening.

One hour and a half later, after a nightmare of arpeggios and scales, Olympia left the music room, intent on getting out of the building as quickly as possible. She glanced at her watch. Almost a quarter to ten! There might still be time to think of another plan, if she could just get back to the hotel. But first, she had to drop the keys in at the Abbot's office.

She was in such a panic to get out of the school that she took a wrong turning, and before she knew what was happening, she had lost her bearings completely. Turning a corner, she found herself baffled by the maze of silent corridors, all identical ancient wood and polished linoleum. To make matters worse, at this time of night the school was as silent as a graveyard, with not a soul in sight to ask for directions.

The sound of footsteps in the distance made her breathe a sigh of relief. So there *was* someone around, who might be able to help her. But the footsteps turned a corner before they reached her, and then receded into the distance.

Well, she would just have to find her own way out of trouble. She had a tongue in her head. All she needed to do was to find someone to ask, a concierge, maybe, or one of the masters, working late in his office. Approaching one of the doors at random, she knocked and waited. There was no answer. And then another. Nothing but the echo of her own heartbeat, deafening in the sepulchral silence. She turned door handles and peered into deserted classrooms. Still nothing that might help her. If she could just find a staircase that would take her down to the ground floor.

She was about to turn and try elsewhere when she caught sight of the large bolted doors at the far end of the corridor, past the long line of offices and classrooms. Maybe they would offer some way out.

She unfastened the bolts and pushed open the door tentatively, unsure of what she might find; and was relieved to discover a flight of stairs leading down to an external door. She hurried down, and tried the door. Mercifully, and miraculously, it was unlocked; and Olympia escaped with heartfelt gratitude into the balmy night air.

To her dismay, she soon realised that she was just as trapped as before, only this time she was confined within the extensive grounds at the back of the school, hemmed in by the high walls which encircled the abbey buildings. She could hear the Paris traffic speeding noisily by, on the other side of the thick stone wall – frustratingly close and yet seemingly unattainable.

Surely there must be a gate somewhere; or another section of wall, low enough to climb over. Olympia threaded her way through the moonlit grounds, following the line of the wall past a rose garden and a small offertory chapel and headed in the direction of the faint sounds she could hear in the distance. If she could find one of the monks, she'd have a lot of explaining to do, but at least they could show her the way out of the school grounds.

As she passed a low stone building behind the main schoolhouse, she caught the yellowish glimmer of torches or lanterns in the distance and, a few moments later, the distinctive flicker of reflections on water. Voices, too. Young voices, hushed yet animated, as though anxious to safeguard some secret, guilty pleasure.

Making her way silently through the trees, she happened upon a sight which took her breath away. There, in the middle of a leafy glade, was a large ornamental lake, its surface gently rippling in the evening breeze.

But it was not the lake itself which made Olympia catch her breath in excitement; nor the circle of lanterns placed on the grass around it, illuminating the scene. For there were beautiful boys swimming in the lake, agile as seals as they slid silently through the dark waters. On the lawns beside the lake older boys sat or lay, their naked bodies as white and perfect as classical statues in the moonlight.

Walking towards them across the grass, Olympia saw all eyes turn to greet her, and her heart began to pound with excitement. She knew that she had at last found what she had been looking for: innocent, inexperienced boys with the bodies and desires of strong young men. As she peeled off her blouse and skirt, and let them fall softly to the ground, the boys' expressions turned from alarm to wonderment and disbelief, the first glimmers of lust brightening their guileless eyes.

And their arms reached out to her in silent longing, begging her to join them in the cool, deep waters; inviting her to usher them with her own sweet skill into the world of men.

Olympia hung on to the end of the rope for a moment longer, then let herself drop to the pavement with a soft thud, landing on hands and knees beside the busy carriageway. Cars and motorbikes sped past along the boulevard, drivers staring in amazement at this slender young woman, climbing out of the Lycée St Siméon in the middle of the night.

Turning round, she almost fell into the arms of a filthy old tramp – the very same one she had seen that first night, on her way back to the Métro station. He was brandishing a bottle of eau-de-vie and leered appreciatively at her as she tried to spring away in disgust.

' – Sacré bleu, M'selle! Is that any way to greet an old friend? How about a little kiss, *hein*?'

Despite Olympia's protests, he succeeded in slipping his free arm round her waist, and drew her close to him. His breath stank of cheap cognac and rancid goose-fat, and Olympia nearly threw up as he stuck his tongue in her mouth. He was excited, too; his hardness was pressing into the flesh of her belly as he ground his pelvis against hers, forcing her against the wall. There could be no doubt that he wanted more than just a kiss.

'Come with me, *chérie*. I know a place, no one will disturb us there.'

As he was fondling her breasts and whispering sweet nothings into her ear, Olympia was moving in for the kill. With a well-aimed knee-jerk, she sent him sprawling backwards on to the pavement, coughing and clasping both hands to his groin.

'Well, well, Mademoiselle Olympia. Not seven virgins, but ten! Another challenge well met and overcome – though I will admit I doubted your abilities for a while. We shall perhaps make a Légionnaire of you yet.'

Olympia felt the warm glow of pride.

'So I have completed the trial to your satisfaction?'

'What matters is not *my* satisfaction, but the Légion's. However, I see no reason why there should be any problem on this occasion.' The messenger placed a tick on his clipboard. 'Now I shall leave you to enjoy the rest of the day. There will be no new trial until tomorrow.'

As he turned to leave, a sudden, wicked impulse overtook Olympia. She grabbed him by the shoulder and turned him round to face her.

'Not so fast, Monsieur. I think you ought to pay for all the terrors you put me through yesterday!'

She strode across to the door and turned the key in the lock.

'What on earth are you doing, Mademoiselle? I have important meetings this afternoon; I must go.'

'I don't think so, Monsieur.'

Olympia held the key just out of arm's reach and, when he seemed about to make a wild grab for it, hitched up her skirt and deftly tucked the key inside her panties, pushing it well up between her love-lips. The cold metal made her shiver with malicious pleasure.

'What . . .?'

'It's perfectly straightforward, Monsieur. If you want the key, you'll have to come and get it.'

'You want me to . . .?'

'Take it from me. Come on! I'm waiting.'

'I see . . .'

There was an intriguing glint in his eyes now. Could this really be the same grey, boring, insignificant flunkey who carried out the will of the Légion so impassively, so unquestioningly?

He took a step closer. Then advanced towards her until he was only inches away. She could feel his hot breath on her cheek as he stroked her bare shoulder with covetous fingertips, then ran his fingers down her smooth throat, into the warm hollow of her cleavage.

His hands were unexpectedly cool on this hot Paris night; and Olympia found his touch rather more pleasurable than she had expected. Perhaps he would not turn out to be entirely uninteresting, after all.

'This is all dreadfully irregular, Mademoiselle. And I'm sure you're perfectly aware of that. After all, what about my impartiality? You wouldn't be trying to bribe me, would you, Olympia Deschamps?'

There was a hint of a smile at the corners of his mouth. 'Really, I should just telephone down to Reception and get them to let me out. Tell them

124

you've accidentally mislaid the key.' His hand
hovered over the phone on the bedside table. 'All
I have to do is pick up the phone and dial zero –
that's it, isn't it, Olympia? Or shall we play your
little game?'

'That's your choice, Monsieur messenger.'

'*Alors, voyons* . . . Why do we not make your
little game a little more interesting? After all, it
would be so easy for me just to slide my fingers
inside you and take the key. Such a simple act
would hold little interest for me.'

Olympia sat down in one of the Louis XV
fauteuils, intrigued now, she crossed her bare
thighs, slowly, so that the messenger would be
sure to get a good, lingering sight of her peach
satin gusset.

'What do you suggest?'

'I suggest a wager. A game of chance,
Mademoiselle.'

He snapped open the lid of his briefcase and
took out a pack of cards.

'Do you play cards, Mademoiselle? I believe strip
poker is an amusing little game.'

Olympia took a sip of chilled white wine, then
lounged back seductively in her chair. She knew
she looked bloody good in the peach satin teddy
and high heels, but it was pretty obvious by now
that the messenger couldn't wait to remove them
from her. Although he was completely naked now,
except for a pair of silk boxer shorts, he was
smirking as he laid his cards on the table in front
of her.

'Four of a kind. Beat that if you can,
Mademoiselle.'

'That's an excellent hand,' conceded Olympia. 'It really is.' Then she laid her cards next to his. 'Pity, really. Royal Straight Flush.'

'But . . .?'

'Yes, I'm afraid so, Monsieur. In spite of your marked cards and your pathetic attempts to cheat me! I hope you're ready to take the consequences.'

She got up from the chair and advanced on him, a playful predator intent on having her sweet revenge. The messenger looked quite taken aback – things clearly weren't going according to plan.

'My game, I think, Monsieur. And you must pay the forfeit.'

'And what might that be?'

'Your body, of course, Monsieur!'

The key long forgotten, she bent over him with a seductive growl, and ran her moist tongue down his naked chest, leaving a trail of wetness over the smooth skin. His nipples were hard, protuberant, and she could not resist taking one into her mouth. It tasted salty, and the powerful, acrid scent of his sweat filled her nostrils, awakening her lust. This might have started as a game, but the time for laughter was long past.

As she bent forward, her full breasts hung heavy over him, like pendulous, juicy fruit; and his hands crept upwards to stroke them, weigh them and test their ripeness. His hands were cool, and his touch both soothed and excited Olympia. She let go of his nipple, and kissed him full on the mouth, her tongue thrusting against his through his parted lips. They jousted playfully for a while, and Olympia gave a little murmur of satisfaction as the messenger began kneading the flesh of her breasts, teasing the nipples with an effectiveness that betrayed his skill.

Warmth surged through her as the messenger took her nipple in his mouth and began sucking at it with a gentle, rhythmic insistence. It felt so, so good, and instinctively she shuffled her feet further apart. She let her hand fall from his shoulder and trace a winding path down his bare torso to his waist, over the smooth tautness of his belly and then down to his thighs.

Teasingly, she ran her fingertips up and down the flesh of his upper thigh, moving ever-closer to the swelling mound of his desire but never quite touching it. His breathing was coming in short, hoarse gasps now, and he was sucking harder and harder at her breast, the fingers of his other hand pinching and kneading her left nipple with such desperate urgency that he held her for an eternity upon the exquisite knife-edge between sweet delight and pain.

At last, sufficient strength returned to her for her to make a move. She hooked her fingers under the waistband of the messenger's black silk boxer shorts, and began tugging them downwards.

'You lost,' she panted, 'and there is still the forfeit to pay, Monsieur.'

He made no attempt at resistance. But who would want to resist the will of the delicious Olympia Deschamps, roused and ready for her prey? He groaned and sank back into the chair as she ripped at the silk and tugged the pants down over his hips, revealing his burgeoning desire.

His manhood was appetisingly large and its fine purple head glistened with a dew-drop of love juice. As it grew fully erect, it seemed at the same time to coax and threaten like some magnificent sun-warmed serpent, uncoiling and ready to strike. The messenger might seem harmless, helpless even; but there was a danger still to be discovered within him – a hidden, seductive darkness that was also the darkness of the Légion d'Amour.

Forbidding him to move, Olympia disappeared momentarily into the bathroom, and went straight to the little wall cupboard where she kept her most costly and exotic cosmetics. A few moments later, she emerged carrying a small bottle of bath oil, some of which she poured into a glass dish on the table. The messenger watched with undisguised interest as she dipped her fingers into the oil, his desire dancing impatiently against his belly.

She knelt between his thighs, and raised her cupped hands over his belly. Then, filling her palm with the warm oil, she tilted it so that the oil ran in a thin golden trickle onto his belly, his groin, his eagerly arching penis.

'Mmm . . . c'est si bon . . . si bon d'avoir tes mains sur le zob.' If this was losing, well, losing wasn't so bad. He had been right in putting the girl's case to the high council of the Légion. She had talent; real talent. Her skilful fingers ran over his sensitive skin again and again, stroking and kneading the warm oil into his firm, willing flesh.

Olympia had always enjoyed massaging her lovers' bodies. Indeed, she had learned the skills of erotic massage early in her life – for the boarding school her father had chosen for her offered an agreeably liberal education.

Lymhurst College was a girls' public school on the edge of the Downs, much favoured by the glitterati. Olympia had shared a dormitory with the daughters of the aristocracy, famous actors, rock stars and even an astronaut. The Lymhurst Foundation also ran a boys' school only a quarter of a mile away, and no one – with the exception of the straightlaced Dr Atherton – minded very much if pupils found their way into each other's beds.

Once a week, on a Wednesday afternoon, the girls attended classes in 'body awareness and personal development'. This could mean anything from modern dance to sex education, but the lessons were never anything other than interesting. Often, she recalled, they had enjoyed nude dancing lessons on the school lawns. On fine, sunny afternoons, they studied life drawing and sculpture in the old summer house beside the lake.

But Olympia's favourite lesson had always been erotic massage. Mixing and warming the massage oil; choosing precisely the right blend to soothe or stimulate; schooling her fingers so that they did the bidding of her partner's body. These were skills which Olympia took to with a natural eagerness and grace which few could match.

Interestingly enough, one of her most cherished early sexual experiences had involved massage. One summer, when she was just sixteen, Olympia had to spend the whole summer at Lymhurst, as her father was out of the country on business. One hot afternoon, she went into the town to buy some fragrant oils for her bath, and on the way back she met Mr Peterson, the new music master.

All the fifth and sixth year girls adored Mr Peterson. He was a real hunk: tall and blond, with sexy broad shoulders and a deliciously tight backside that rippled with a hint of muscle when he

walked. Not at all what you'd call a typical music
master, Darius Peterson played rugby, cricket,
squash and swam twenty lengths every morning
before breakfast, and still managed to play the
violin like an angel possessed by demons.

Olympia had always thought she was immune
to him. She was much too grown up to have
crushes on her teachers. Besides, he didn't seem
to show much interest in any of the girls. She'd
even wondered idly if he was gay. He did have
that hard, perfectly-proportioned body that seems
to turn some gay men on. Secretly, in the privacy
of her own dreams, Olympia had to acknowledge
that it turned her on, too.

On this particular afternoon, Olympia was irritated rather than pleased to meet Mr Peterson. She
wanted to be alone, and here he was, being chatty
and annoyingly affable. To her surprise, she
allowed herself to be talked into going for a walk
on the Downs, and she couldn't help chuckling to
herself as she thought how green with envy all her
schoolfriends would be if they only knew.

At first, the walk was tiresome, and Olympia
could hardly wait for them to get back to the
village so that she could make her excuses and get
back on the bus to Lymhurst. But little by little,
she relaxed in his company and when he suggested sitting down for a rest, she did not refuse.

They settled down on the warm, dry grass, in
the shade of a stand of copper beech trees. In the
distance, racehorses were thundering across the
gallops, the beat of their hooves on the dry turf
like the pounding of Olympia's heartbeat. With a
start, she realised that Darius Peterson was now

sitting *very* close beside her, and his fingers were gently stroking her arm.

'Drink?'

The music master opened his rucksack and took out a bottle of mineral water. Gratefully, Olympia accepted it and took a long, luxurious draught. It was invigoratingly cool, and the bubbles felt like a thousand tiny pin-pricks as they burst on her tongue.

As Peterson drank, she watched his muscular throat contract, and could not suppress a little shiver of excitement as she looked at his bare, golden shoulders and muscular thighs, perfect and golden in sleeveless cotton vest and crisp, white shorts.

He put down the bottle and screwed on the cap. With a grin, he made a playful grab for Olympia's bag.

'What have you got in there, eh? I've always wanted to know what you girls carry in your handbags. What is it that makes them so bloody heavy, that's what I want to know.'

'Put that down! Give it me back at once!'

'Now, let's see. Paper tissues, lipstick, aspirins, empty condom packet. What's this, then?'

He held up the bottle of fragrant oil, and Olympia felt herself reddening with annoyance.

'Haven't you ever seen a bottle of bath oil before?'

He unscrewed the top, and breathed in the fragrance.

'Hmm. Musky, orangey, sweet. This is wasted in your bath, Olympia. I can think of much more interesting places for it to go.'

He poured a few drops into his hand, then

reached out and smoothed them over Olympia's bare arm. She shivered with involuntary pleasure at his firm, knowing touch.

'Would you like me to show you what to do with this oil, Olympia?'

She did not reply: she had no need to. Already her body was singing with delight at Darius Peterson's audacious touch, and as he slid his hand up underneath the hem of her blouse, she sank back on to the soft earth, surrendering utterly to the force of his will.

He unfastened her bra with a single, deft movement, and pushed it upwards, baring her breasts to his insistent caresses. The warm silky-smoothness of the oil erected her nipples and moistened the gusset of her panties with a little rush of love-juice.

As he massaged her with one hand, he used the other to unfasten her clothes. At the back of her mind, Olympia couldn't help worrying that here, in the open air, someone might come past and see them; but pleasure was too strong for her, and Peterson's skill allayed all her fears. Her entire world was the smoothing hand, the caressing fingertips.

He eased off her skirt and panties, and she stretched out on the grass before him, naked and relaxed. When he poured more oil on to her belly, and began massaging her pubis, her thighs seemed to part instinctively, opening up the flower of her womanhood.

His fingers slid between her thighs, and gently parting her love-lips, he penetrated the very heart of her intimacy. She cried out, unable to hold back her pleasure as his fingers worked on her, the

132

sweet, slick oil lubricating and warming her with a joyous insistence.

The pleasure was almost unbearable, for he had the skill to bring her again and again to the brink of ecstasy, and yet deny her the moment of ultimate fulfilment. Tears sprang to her eyes as he played her body, as the maestro plays an exquisite instrument, and she writhed in an agony of sweet sensations as his fingers struck still sweeter symphonies from her willing flesh.

'Give it to me, give it to me.'

Her desperate moans beseeched him for mercy. And at last, he took pity on her and began undressing. Underneath his shorts and T-shirt, Darius Peterson was naked; and his body was even more beautiful than she had imagined. It was obvious that he shaved his body hair, for his skin was sleek and smooth and golden, showing off his musculature to best advantage. But his greatest beauty was his phallus: strong and magnificently formed, and below it, two heavy globes in a velvety golden pouch, full and juicy and ready for love.

He upended the bottle of sweet oil into his hand, and let it trickle luxuriously over his loins, massaging it into the flesh with eager, expert hands.

'Now I am ready for you, Olympia. Are you ready for me?'

'Oh yes . . .' she heard herself gasp. 'Do it to me . . . now.'

He slid into her like a hot knife into butter; the hard perfection of his engorged member perfectly complemented by the slick, fragrant oil which clung to him like a silken glove.

They rode together on the sun-warmed grass; and overhead, the afternoon sunlight blazed down

133

through the coppery leaves, casting a dazzling shadow-play upon their glistening, naked bodies.

They came together in a sunburst of colour and light, and the thunder of horses' hooves on the sunbaked grass matched the breathless thumping of their hearts.

And now here she was in a Paris hotel room, massaging her own special blend of sweet oils into the messenger's dancing flesh. He was an appreciative subject, but Olympia's own body was crying out now to be touched, caressed, explored – to be taught to sing as it had once done on the sunlit Downs.

As though reading her thoughts, the messenger suddenly pulled her forward, so that she fell on top of him, his hardness trying to burrow its way into her bare belly. She giggled as he fumbled with the buttons on her teddy, trying to resist him yet praying that her resistance would be overcome.

With a sharp tug, he ripped open the buttons, and the tiny triangle of peach satin fell away, revealing her red-gold pubic curls in all their glory.

As she grew ever-wetter with desire, the key slid out of her and fell soundlessly on to the carpet; but they paid it no heed. Neither was interested in that part of the game any more.

His arms were around her now, pulling her on top of him so that his hardness nudged against the moist, hot pleasure-garden between her thighs.

'Take me!' cried Olympia, as his well-oiled hardness slid smoothly into the very depths of her. 'Take me now, and never, never stop . . .'

Chapter Seven

'This could get me into a great deal of trouble,' remarked the messenger as he straightened his tie and slipped on his suit jacket. 'I must get back to my office straight away; and let us hope no one has noticed that I have spent an entire day and night with you. Such a scandal might well invalidate the trials.'

Olympia smiled, and stretched out, cat-like, on the bed.

'What's the hurry? We could spend today in bed, as well.'

'I thought you wanted to become the first female member of the Légion d'Armour.'

'Yes, of course; but . . .'

'Then you must face today's trial.'

He opened his briefcase, and took out a card.

'Up to now, your performance has been undeniably satisfactory, Mademoiselle Olympia. I myself can testify to your indefatigable enthusiasm. But the Légion has devised some challenging trials for your sexual abilities.'

He handed Olympia the card, and she read it with mounting interest.

'Today, you must use both your sexual and entrepreneurial skills,' ran the message. 'You must deliver an erotic porcelain statuette to the Galérie Sainte Marie, and sell it to the gallery's director, using all the skills at your disposal to persuade him.'

Olympia smiled at the messenger.

'That is not such a terrible challenge!' she exclaimed. 'I'm a talented and experienced art dealer. I can sell art to anyone . . . if it's worth buying.'

The messenger raised his hand to silence her.

'That is not in doubt,' he agreed. 'You are a skilful saleswoman, and the piece which you must sell is of the highest quality – unique, I daresay. But there are two essential facts which you should bear in mind. First, the statuette depicts explicit sexual acts. Second, the Galérie Sainte Marie purchases and displays only works of religious and devotional art, and its director is none other than Monsignor Giacomo Testi – a Jesuit priest.'

After breakfast and a little therapeutic shopping in the Avenue Montaigne, Olympia went over to see Joachim at his studio. When she got there, she found him busily packing his paintings for the trip to England.

'Do you think I should send this one? Or this? I simply cannot decide which of these paintings ought to go into the exhibition. Sometimes, I think not a single one of them is good enough, and I should burn them all! What am I going to do, Olympia?' He threw up his hands in despair, and flopped down on the old, battered sofa.

Olympia surveyed the chaos and laughed.

'If only all my artists had the same problem! Most of them have trouble finding half a dozen pictures that are good enough to exhibit. And you've got dozens! Do you know, one of my painters once threw his entire year's output out of the window, poured turps all over it and set fire to it in the back garden!'

She kissed Joachim tenderly, perched herself on his knee and ran her hands through his blond, wavy hair.

'Isn't there anything we could do to calm you down?'

'Well . . .' He returned her kiss with a sly grin, and slid a paint-spattered hand over her pale blue miniskirt. 'I'm open to suggestions.'

Olympia pulled the silk vest off over her head, and in a second Joachim was upon her, showering kisses on her bare breasts and fumbling with the side-button on her skirt.

His youthful ardour was just what she needed, and she relaxed in his arms, letting a multi-coloured wave of sensations wash over her. Joachim was special; she was going to miss him like crazy when he left for London. But for now, she would forget about tomorrow and just enjoy the passion of the moment. He was so young, so strong, so exciting, and she laughed delightedly as he gathered her up in his arms and carried her off into his little attic bedroom.

The sheets were grimy and rumpled, but Olym-

137

pia couldn't have cared less. All she wanted was to feel the warmth of this eager young animal, burning into her. She tore off his shirt as he planted kisses on her breasts, her belly, her throat; and he struggled out of his jeans, hungry for her with the desperate hunger of youth – so easily aroused, so difficult to assuage.

He wanted to throw himself on top of her, enter her without any preliminaries, but Olympia slowed him down, made him delay his satisfaction.

'It will be better . . . more fun for both of us.'

'But I want you now, Olympia. I want you so much.'

'I want you too, Joachim. But I don't just want you to enjoy me like your eleven o'clock casse-croûte in the Café Rodolphe. I want you to make love to me, Joachim. Real love. Here – taste me here.'

She took hold of his hand, and slid it between her thighs, guiding it to her love-button.

'Kiss me there, Joachim. Kiss me and make me come.'

He slid down her body, leaving a trail of moist kisses, and parted her love-lips with gentle fingers. His wriggling tongue, at first hesitant, quickly learned the paths of pleasure under Olympia's expert guidance; and she writhed delightedly under his determined assaults. As he licked her, she wound his hair round her fingers and ran desperate nails down his smooth, golden back, leaving little red tiger-stripes.

'Darling,' she breathed. 'My own darling Joachim.'

And then it happened. Pleasure turned to

138

ecstasy, and she felt herself opening up like an exotic orchid that blooms only once in a hundred years.

'I'm coming, I'm coming!' she cried, and, clutching his back, she surrendered to the tyranny of desire.

When she had recovered, she rolled him on to his back and straddled him like a trusted steed. He was half laughing, half crying with need for her, and when she took his beautiful hard penis and let it slide up into the warm, wet depths of her, he gave a cry of anguished need.

She rode him long and hard, refusing to allow him to come too soon to pleasure; but youthful lust is a tyrannical master, and he was full of love-juice for her, full as a ripe fruit, its skin about to burst with sun-warmed July sap. With a great groan of blissful release, he spurted into her and she fell laughing on his belly as her own orgasm took her to a sunlit plateau of ecstasy.

Afterwards, they lay curled up on Joachim's bed, listening to one another's breathing, and to the sounds of traffic, floating up from the street below.

'I have to go soon,' breathed Olympia, nibbling Joachim's ear playfully. 'You know . . . business.'

'No, surely not. Why can't you stay here? *Pourquoi, chérie*? Why is it that you must leave me?'

'It's just that there's something really important that I have to do, that's all.'

'So you think I am not important, then?'

'Of course you are, but . . .'

'Then stay, Olympia. I want to make love to you all over again.'

Wishing that she did not have to resist the tyranny of her desire, she kissed him silently, then slid off the bed and began to get dressed. She longed to tell him about her quest; about her burning desire to right the wrong done to her father. Longed to be able to ask him for help. But she could hardly tell him the real reason why she was in Paris.

Olympia turned the corner into Rue Keller and walked down past a parade of smart shops. The porcelain group of figures was much heavier than she had expected, and she clutched the box to her tightly, trying not to think about the horrendous consequences if she dropped it on the pavement.

The Galérie Sainte Marie was situated in between a high-class couturier and a religious bookshop, and Olympia's heart sank as she walked towards it. A single glance confirmed what the messenger had said: every single item in the window was on a religious theme; she could see icons, paintings of the Passion, religious statuary, exquisite jewelled reliquaries and a set of rosary beads. What on earth would Monsignor Testi want with a tableau of erotic statuettes?

Nevertheless, a challenge was a challenge, and Olympia guessed that there must be some purpose behind it. Perhaps once she was inside the shop, events would guide her.

She pressed the doorbell, and an elderly woman's voice crackled through the entryphone: *'C'est de la part de qui?'*

'Mademoiselle Olympia Deschamps,' replied Olympia. 'I have a fine piece of porcelain which I would like the Monsignor to see.'

A buzzer sounded, and Olympia pushed open the door. Inside, the shop was filled with the musty scent of old incense and polished wood. An old woman clad in rusty black shuffled forwards out of the gloom.

'Mademoiselle?'

'I would like to see Monsignor Testi, please. I have a piece I would like to show him.'

'The Monsignor is a very busy man. Perhaps if you were to show the piece to me . . .?'

Olympia clutched the box to her more tightly. There was no way she was showing 'The Triumph of Venus' to this respectable old woman.

'Er . . . no, thank you, Madame. It's most important that the Monsignor sees it personally. I have come all the way from London with it, you see.'

'Very well. I will find him for you. But I cannot guarantee that he will agree to see you.'

To Olympia's relief, the old crone hobbled off into a back room, without insisting on seeing the statuette. Five minutes later she was back, this time with a tall, middle-aged priest with a sweep of jet-black hair and round, horn-rimmed spectacles perched on his nose. The old woman backed away obsequiously, and disappeared into the back room, closing the door quietly behind her.

'I believe you have something you wish to show me, Mademoiselle?'

Olympia swallowed hard.

'I . . . that is . . . yes. A porcelain statuette. That is to say, a rather interesting porcelain group – one of the lesser-known eighteenth-century works from the Meissen factory.'

She opened the lid of the box, brushed away the shredded paper and gently lifted out the porcelain figures, mounted on a polished mahogany base.

All at once, she felt horribly embarrassed. How could she have been silly enough to bring this obscenity into a gallery of religious art?

She placed the piece on the table, and stood back. There was no doubt about it, it was pornographic. The group depicted a naked man on his knees before a large-breasted nude woman, who was parting her love-lips to allow his tongue to enter her. Meanwhile, a ferocious woman was standing behind him, raising a wicked-looking cat-o'-nine-tails to thrash his already red and bleeding back.

The Monsignor stared open-mouthed at the porcelain group. There was an alarmingly long silence, during which Olympia considered grabbing the statuette, and making a run for it.

'*En bien . . . oui.*' He took off his spectacles and wiped them on the sleeve of his *soutane*, before turning his searching gaze on Olympia. 'But, Mademoiselle, what makes you imagine that I would wish to see such . . . ordure? Surely you can see that this is a gallery of religious art?'

Olympia squirmed, but could not allow herself to weaken.

'I was told that you might have a certain personal interest in the subject-matter.'

It was a shot in the dark, but it provoked an interesting reaction.

'I see.' He cast a furtive glance behind him, and turned a key in the door to the back room. Then he glanced quickly out of the front door of the shop, and turned the sign to read '*Fermé*'. 'Well, this is by no means the type of *oeuvre* which I would generally consider suitable for the Galérie Sainte Marie. However, it is an exceptional piece.

142

Perhaps we should discuss the matter further in private. Please follow me. I keep my personal collection in the strongroom, downstairs.'

He switched on a wall light, and Olympia saw a winding wrought-iron staircase, spiralling down into the basement of the shop. At once she felt apprehensive, but this was not the time to discover the meaning of caution. Gingerly, she stepped on to the first step and followed Monsignor Testi down into the darkness.

They passed through heavy, combination-locked doors, and through into a gloomy basement. Only when the doors were closed behind them, did the priest click on the light switch. Suddenly, it occurred to Olympia that, should he so choose, the priest could quite easily imprison her down here, appropriate the Meissen statuette, and no one would ever know what had happened to her. No one but the Légion d'Amour.

'Place the tableau upon the table, my dear. I wish to examine it more closely.'

Olympia obeyed, and the priest examined it at some length with a jeweller's eyeglass. But Olympia was not watching the priest. She was looking around this curious cellar storeroom, which seemed to hold a whole host of intriguing mysteries. The walls were lined with display cases, the glass front of each obstructed by a hanging curtain of midnight blue velvet.

In the centre of the room stood an antique wooden *prie-Dieu*, with a number of highly unusual features. Instead of a padded base for the penitent to kneel on, there was a double row of cruel spikes, designed to cause the most extreme pain. And attached to the top rail of the *prie-Dieu* were a studded collar and a pair of heavy iron manacles and chains. Olympia imagined what it would be like to be chained to such an instrument of torture, and shivered with vicarious discomfort.

'The piece is genuine,' observed the priest, putting down his eyeglass. 'And exquisitely made. Do you see how beautifully painted are the smears of blood on the victim's wounded back? It is certainly a valuable collector's item. But such a secular piece . . . I wonder that you should think it of any interest to one such as I.'

Olympia did not answer, but turned towards the darkened display cases.

'No, Mademoiselle. *Absolument non!* I forbid it!'

But she ignored the Monsignor's command, and pushed away the curtain which shrouded the first of the display cases. Inside lay a long, coiled leather bullwhip, marked here and there with patches of rusty brown which Olympia realised with horror must be dried blood. She wheeled round and cast a questioning glance at Monsignor Testi. In a moment he was by her side.

'It belonged to St Ignatius Loyola himself, Mademoiselle Deschamps. That is his own sacred blood which stains the lash. Is that not a wondrous sight? To stand witness to the glorious redemption of an earthly sinner?'

He led her to the next case.

'Arrows from the martyrdom of St Sebastian. Birch twigs used to martyr the sweet, soft flesh of St Agnes. You see, Mademoiselle, without pain there can be no redemption. And in order for punishment, it is first necessary to commit transgressions. We must first commit sin, if we are to know the incomparable joy of penance.'

144

'But, isn't that . . .?'

'*Oui, Mademoiselle*. I follow the sacred teachings of the blessed monk Rasputin.'

Stunned, she looked into his eyes, and saw a mad ecstasy there. Was it too late to make her excuses, to run away?

He was taking one of the whips out of its case now, caressing it between slender, artistic fingers; gazing lovingly at the porcelain 'Triumph of Venus', as though it held some secret and essential truth which he longed to bring to life.

With a supreme effort of will, Olympia forced herself to stop panicking, and think. She had been sent here by the Légion to use her powers of sexual persuasion, not to lie down and accept whatever the curious Monsignor had planned for her. And whatever that might be, she wasn't about to submit to the discipline of the bullwhip.

In a single, sudden movement she snatched the whip from the priest's hands. Its handle sat surprisingly snugly in her hand, and a new excitement coursed through her veins as she made the tip of the lash slice through the air with a loud and satisfying crack.

Monsignor Testi stared at her as though transfixed before some divine – or diabolical vision. Seizing the moment, Olympia prepared to act her part to perfection.

'Sinner!' she cried. 'Down on the floor, you miserable, sinful wretch. I want to see you crawl. I want to hear you beg for forgiveness.'

With a sob that might have been distress or pleasure, the Jesuit fell to his knees on the dusty cellar floor.

'I said down!' barked Olympia. 'On your belly,

like the filthy serpent you are. I want to see you eat dirt.'

The priest sank to the floor, assisted by a savage flick of the bullwhip which caught him on the shoulders and threw him forward on to his face.

'Now crawl, serpent; crawl on your belly in the dust.'

Her hissed command admitted no possibility of disobedience. Moaning softly, the priest began grovelling and squirming on the cellar floor. Olympia guided his progress with deft little flicks of the whip, and a few well-aimed strokes of a supple cane she found lying inside one of the glass cases.

Once, twice, she made him crawl round the cellar, until at last she tired of the game and decided to give it a new and more original turn. The *prie-Dieu* was so conveniently near, so delightfully theatrical; and the keys were still in the iron manacles!

'Crawl to the *prie-Dieu*, wretch. You must be properly punished for your sinful pleasure. How else do you expect to attain the bliss of heavenly salvation?'

The unfortunate priest obeyed, with more eagerness than distress, Olympia noted with interest. When he reached the *prie-Dieu* she dragged him up on to his knees and commanded him to kneel on the double row of spikes as she forced his head into the constricting leather collar. Although little more than iron studs, she knew the spikes beneath his knees must be causing him the most intense discomfort, and the knowledge somehow pleased and excited her. Never before had she been so supremely the mistress of a man's pleasure and pain.

146

She clicked the manacles on to the priest's wrist, and locked them. He made no attempt to resist, and it was obvious that Olympia's suspicions about his sexual preferences had been entirely correct. This was a man who enjoyed not inflicting pain, but receiving it. Here was a profoundly sensual man, obsessed with the need to atone for sins he did not even want to stop committing. Well, Olympia had no intention of disappointing him.

She stood back and took a long, hard look at her victim. He looked uncomfortable, embarrassed even, but where were the extremes of suffering that she sensed he craved so desperately? She looked deep into his eyes and saw only a lewd excitement, the anticipation of imminent sensual gratification. Well, before gratification must come pain; before celestial bliss, an inferno of everlasting torment.

Another glass case furnished a shiny-bladed knife with a wickedly sharp point. Olympia made sure that Monsignor Testi had had a really good look at the wafer-thin steel before she slashed off his clothes with it, using wild, sweeping strokes that must have seemed desperately reckless as they skimmed the delicate surface of his skin. But Olympia was in control, and enjoying every ounce of her power.

A final slash of the knife cut away the last threads of the *soutane*, and Olympia saw that, underneath, the priest was wearing a hair shirt. She tore that away, too, and was intrigued to see how the garment had scratched and irritated the sensitive skin. Clearly this was a man who was accustomed to discomfort, welcoming it as others welcomed kisses and caresses: she would have to be imaginative and energetic if she was to excite him and enslave his spirit.

A few strokes of the bullwhip awoke pain and lust in her victim, and she taunted him mercilessly as, with each new surge of pain, his manhood grew ever more erect, straining for the release which she knew she must deny him.

'First the sin, then the redemption through pain,' breathed Olympia, remembering the priest's unorthodox philosophy.

'Mercy!' The priest's voice was very different now; no longer booming and authoritative, it had shrunk to a feeble whisper, hoarse and wheedling. Olympia surveyed him with growing disdain, despising this weak-minded hypocrite who could not practise what he preached.

'No mercy,' she barked. 'I want to see the disgusting depths of sin into which you are capable of falling.'

She took off her jacket and turned to lay it neatly over the back of a chair, and her eye lighted on the porcelain group still standing in the middle of the table, lit by the pale yellow glow from the concealed wall lighting. A serious collector, this Monsignor Testi, mused Olympia; he cares about his exhibits enough to ensure they are not damaged in any way. In the background, the dull hum of the air-conditioning bore witness to the controlled atmosphere necessary for such rare and exquisite artefacts.

The 'Triumph of Venus' seemed to burn with an inner fire, light glowing through the translucent breast of the angry goddess as she prepared to bring down the lash again and again upon her victim's bloody back. His eyes were full of a strange intensity as pain and desire mingled in his helpless body, and he pressed his lips once more to the golden bush of pubic curls. A halo of light seemed to surround the blonde head of the girl who stood before him, left hand clasping the back of his head as his tongue penetrated deeper and deeper into her most secret garden. Head thrown back, she was laughing with a mad joy, and her puckered nipples testified to the depth of her pleasure.

An idea came to Olympia. Slowly and seductively, she began to undress. The priest started to groan with anguish as, little by little, she uncovered the beauty of her body to him. He strained to reach out to her, to touch the perfect gold of her smooth skin; but the manacles and dog collar held him fast; and he was her helpless, hopeless victim, utterly abandoned to his lust.

She undid the little pearl buttons of her blouse one by one, with painful slowness. There seemed to be dozens of them, and they defied haste. The blouse was tight and semi-diaphanous, like a second skin of fine, white cotton lawn. It seemed to blaze against her golden skin as the fabric fell away, little by agonising little.

'*Pour l'amour de Dieu* . . . ,' groaned Monsignor Testi.

'Silence, wretch!'

She silenced him with a sharp blow from the whip across the shoulders; not hard enough to cause real pain, but enough to startle and burn. He gasped, and stared at her with round, frightened eyes. Frightened and excited.

'*Pas un mot*; not a word? Do you understand?

Not a word, no matter what I do, no matter what the pain. Or it will be the worse for you.'

She peeled off the blouse, folded it neatly and laid it across her jacket on the chair. Excitement was puckering her nipples, warming her belly; excitement at tantalising this hopeless, helpless man, playing his weakness like an old violin, making him wait for his gratification like a dog whining for a titbit.

Next, the brassiere; a tiny scrap of lace and elastic that seemed to fall away to nothing as she unfastened the clasp. Beneath, her breasts were full and firm and golden – that even tan that showed the priest how Olympia Deschamps loved to walk naked in the summer sunshine. She smiled to herself as she thought how he would react to that same, golden tan on her belly and buttocks.

She unfastened the button on the pale blue miniskirt, and pulled down the zip with a sound like a little sigh. Wriggling her hips, she eased the skintight fabric over her hips and stepped out of it, placing the folded skirt on top of the blouse on the chair.

Now she was naked, save for her panties, shoes and a pair of playful lacy stockings, decorated with pictures of cupids. She walked towards the *prie-Dieu* and stood inches away, just out of his reach. He struggled desperately to touch, to kiss, to caress; but she defied him, loving the sense of power over him.

'*Je vous en prie,*' he begged.

'No!'

Again the whip cracked down on his bare flesh, this time leaving an angry red weal across shoulders and back. He gave a long groan and closed his eyes in pain, but his penis was dancing with pleasure, its tip glistening with love-dew that Olympia longed to taste.

For this was a torment for Olympia, as much as it was for Monsignor Testi. All her senses screamed for her to suck him dry, then stroke and tease him back into hardness and ride him; ride him until they cried out together at the peak of their twin ecstasy. Only the knowledge of the trial that she must pass held her back, and made her keep on playing out this pretty, tormenting, titillating charade.

At last she took a step forward, so that her belly was pressed up against Testi's face. Then she inserted her fingers under the waistband of her little white lace panties and pulled it slowly downwards, revealing the seamless tanned skin beneath. For Olympia was a lady who liked to bare every inch of her flesh to the sun.

She pulled down the panties and stepped out of them, then pressed the moist triangle of her pubis against the priest's face. He gave a little sigh, and when he opened his eyes Olympia was astonished to see that he was weeping. Big, slow tears were trickling down his cheeks as the secret fragrance of her sex awakened his guilty desires. Guilty, but all too willing.

Olympia bent and grabbed hold of his chin, jerking up his head so that he was forced to look into her angry green eyes.

'Lick me, pleasure me, you little wretch,' she commanded him. 'Show me how you sin; how you dream of taking your pleasure in the depths of corruption. And you'd better do it well,' she added, 'or your punishment will be all the more severe.'

She pressed her red-gold curls against Testi's face, and pulled apart her love-lips to let him in. His tongue was hot and eager – so eager that she almost cried out with the suddenness and the urgency of his touch.

He was a skilful and instinctive lover, searching out her clitoris in a second, and titillating it with delicate little flicks of his tongue that drove her wild with lust. Here she was, supposedly playing the cruel dominatrix, and her slave had her utterly in his thrall, if he only dared believe it. She forced herself to appear cool-headed.

'Oui, oui . . . passable. Ça y est. No! Harder, you miserable creature. Or I shall flay the skin from your despicable body.'

He obeyed every command with the eagerness of a small boy, desperate to please the beautiful young teacher who has brought him into a whole new world of sensations he does not yet even understand. He lapped at her as though drinking from an inexhaustible spring of honeydew; and with each touch of his tongue-tip, Olympia felt another flood of the precious fluid welling up inside her and gushing out in a miniature waterfall of desire.

The effort of remaining impassive was almost unbearable. She wanted to cry out, sing, weep with pleasure, but she knew she must not. The orgasm was almost upon her, and she must enjoy it as silently as her victim, surrendering to the tryanny of her pleasure.

'Harder, faster, wretch; do it to me, now. I command you!'

Testi's hot, muscular tongue teased the hyper-sensitive flesh around her clitoris, and she knew she could hold out no longer. Clenching her teeth to suppress the howl of pleasure she could not allow herself, Olympia gave a silent sigh of desire, abandoning herself to the dizziness of her climax: a tumbling cascade of pleasure that left her dazzled and exhilarated.

As the waves of delight ebbed away, she looked down and saw Testi's eyes gazing up at her — pleading, begging, praying for her approval.

She pulled away. Her juices were dripped down his chin in clear, glistening trickles.

'Filth!' she cried, picking up the whip and bringing it down again upon his shoulders. 'Is this how you go about your devotions? I can see that we shall have to teach you the meaning of true penitence.' She crouched down in front of him, lowering her face to his. Sweat was trickling down his forehead, and his hair was matted into little black rat's-tails. 'Have you sinned, wretch?'

'*Oui, oui, Maîtresse!* I have committed a terrible sin.'

'What sin have you committed? *Vite, vite!* Tell me at once, wretch!'

'I . . . I have committed the sins of lust and fornication, Maîtresse. And I truly deserve to be punished for my sins.'

'And how shall we punish you? What penance shall you have to bear?' She hardly needed to ask him. For already she knew the answer he would give.

He lowered his eyes, and she saw that he was trembling. When he answered her, it was in a hoarse whisper, full of awe and sensual excitement.

'Mortification of the flesh, Maîtresse. That is the punishment that such heinous sins demand. The only punishment worthy of such terrible crimes against righteousness. You must mortify the flesh that has committed the sin – purge it of its impurity through pain and humiliation.'

Olympia smiled, a thin-lipped smile of satisfaction. So this curious dilettante priest was indeed a pathetic masochist, as she had guessed. Well, he would have the satisfaction he craved. After all, wasn't it only fair to reward him for the pleasure he had given her?

She walked round behind him and raised the whip again, this time bringing it down with real energy upon his naked back. He whimpered as the cruel leather of the bullwhip cut into his soft flesh; but a sharp command from his mistress silenced him, and he bit into the back of his hand to stifle his cries of distress, and pleasure.

Again and again the bullwhip flashed through the air; and Olympia realised that she too was growing more and more excited by the spectacle of her power. As she whipped her victim, she slid her left hand between her thighs and began rubbing at her clitoris, exciting herself once again to a peak of excitement.

'Suffer, wretch! Suffer for your sin!'

With each stroke of the lash, Testi writhed in his bonds and grew more and more agitated. Olympia saw that his manhood was straining for release; and she began directing the whip at his buttocks, so that its cruel tip snaked between his parted

154

thighs and bit into the delicate flesh of his velvet pouch.

'Surrender to the pain! To the pain and the pleasure of pain.'

At last the torment was too much for Testi, and with a tremendous howl of anguish he gave himself up to the humiliation of his pleasure. His semen spurted out in hot, white jets, falling to the ground where it formed opalescent pools. The sight of his surrender was all Olympia needed to push her over the edge into delicious oblivion, and she caressed herself into a second, blissful climax.

When she looked down at Testi, he was slumped over the *prie-Dieu*, panting and utterly spent. After a few moments, he opened his eyes.

'You may free me now, Mademoiselle. It was an agreeable interlude.'

Olympia chuckled.

'Not so fast, Monsignor Testi. First, there is the small matter of "The Triumph of Venus". I should so much like to see it displayed in the window of the Galérie Sainte Marie.'

'But, this is a gallery of religious and devotional art, Mademoiselle. I cannot possibly. I might perhaps be persuaded to purchase it for my private collection, but for the Galérie! *Non*! It is unthinkable!'

'Such a pity,' sighed Olympia. 'I had hoped you were a reasonable man. And now it seems I shall have to resort to other methods of persuasion.' She turned towards the door of the cellar. 'Now, Joachim! Now!'

The door swung open, and the silhouette of a figure appeared in the doorway. A dazzling brightness flashed once, twice, a dozen times in rapid succession.

'Monsieur Joachim has a very artistic touch with a camera,' explained Olympia with a smile. 'I am sure the pictures will be tremendously . . . instructive. And of course, the newspapers and magazines are sure to be interested in publishing photographs of a Jesuit father at his very personal devotions.'

'*Non!* Mademoiselle, you cannot!'

'Oh, but I can, Monsignor. And I shall – if you do not agree to buy "The Triumph of Venus" and put it on display in the window of the Galérie Sainte Marie immediately. It is a simple enough choice to make, Monsignor. A little awkwardness, or a very great deal of embarrassment.'

There was a short silence.

'Very well, Mademoiselle,' sighed the Monsignor. 'I see there is no alternative for me but to agree to your demands. You are a most persuasive young lady. But I must have your word . . . the photographs and the negatives . . .'

'They will be returned to you as soon as the piece goes on display,' promised Olympia. 'You have my word on that. And Joachim's.'

She nodded to Joachim, and he ducked out of the room, back in the shadows. Olympia heard his footsteps going back up the stairs towards the shop and the door to the boulevard. She was glad she had involved him now – telling him just enough to be able to help her, without giving away the secret of her quest.

She freed the priest, and watched him cover his shame with one of the black *soutanes* he kept in a cupboard in the strongroom.

156

'I shall be back later this afternoon, Monsignor,' announced Olympia, buttoning up her blouse and turning to leave. 'If I were you, I should arrange to have "The Triumph of Venus" on display. If not, I cannot be responsible for the consequences.'

With that, she turned on her heel and disappeared back up the stairs towards the shop, leaving behind her a very bemused and considerably chastened Monsignor Testi.

Chapter Eight

Olympia and Joachim spent a couple of hours at the Grand Louvre, admiring the Watteaus and Fragonards, and then decided to indulge in a little clandestine fun.

'Believe it or not, I've never done anything quite like this before!' giggled Olympia as they slipped past the watchful eye of the gallery attendant and through the door of the gentlemen's *toilettes*.

'Don't worry,' replied Joachim with a grin, pushing her into one of the cubicles and sliding home the bolt. 'I had – how you say – a mis-spent youth! When you're a penniless student, *ma chère*, with nowhere to go . . . well, you find ways of making things happen. I have done this many times and *jamais de problèmes!*'

'Oh you have, have you?' Olympia relaxed as he pressed her up against the flimsy dividing wall, thankful that they were apparently the only people in the toilets. 'Quite the little Lothario, aren't we?'

He silenced her giggles with a kiss, and she

retaliated by unbuttoning his jeans and sliding her hand through the flies until it made sweet, vibrant contact with his swelling hardness.

'I want you, *chérie*,' he breathed, holding her very close. 'Want you now.'

'I want you too,' she murmured. 'But I don't see how we're going to—'

His kisses ended her protest; his hands exploring the warmth of her willing body beneath the flimsy cotton blouse and skintight skirt.

'Watching you tormenting that horny old priest . . . Watching him licking you out . . . That's the most exciting thing I've ever seen, *sans blague*. Just where did you learn to do things like that, Miss Olympia Deschamps? Is that what they teach you at English public school?'

She laughed, and began gently caressing his shaft, sliding her other hand down between his thighs, to cradle his scrotum.

'I had good teachers, sweetheart; that's true. And I'll be your teacher if you'll let me.'

'But Olympia, why were you in that cellar with him? Why did you need me to take those photos? You never explain anything to me.'

'I can't tell you that, Joachim. Not yet. But soon, if things work out the way I want them to. Well, if I can I'll tell you, I promise.' She returned his kisses, rubbing harder at his shaft. 'Can't we forget it for now? Can't we just have fun?'

'*Doucement*, *chérie*,' whispered Joachim. 'Much more of that, and you'll have me coming in your hand instead of your . . .' He pulled her close to him. 'Let me have you. Now. I cannot wait another moment!'

He turned round and sat down on the lavatory

seat, pulling down his jeans so that they were round his knees.

'Sit on me, Olympia. Let me slide into you.'

She lowered herself on to his upraised shaft, delighting in the way it slid effortlessly between her love-lips, into the very depths of her; until at last it was pressing against the neck of her womb.

'Do it to me. Do it to me, darling,' gasped Joachim. And Olympia began raising and lowering herself, aided by his strong hands around her waist. Up and down, again and again, he slid in and out of her and she knew she must keep silent or someone would guess what was going on inside the cubicle. She could hear people moving about outside. But there was no way she was going to stop, not now that she had him inside her. She marvelled at the way he could excite her: this young, quite inexperienced young artist whose animal passion so aroused her.

His finger slipped around and between her thighs, bringing her suddenly to an agonizing climax made all the more intense by the need to keep absolute silence. As it was. Joachim gave a little groan of pleasure as he spurted into the depths of her sex.

They stayed there for a long time, locked together in passion's embrace; both of them desperately tempted just to stay there and begin all over again.

'I must go,' gasped Olympia, making a determined attempt to be strong. After all, she had the trials to think of. 'I really must. I said I'd go back to the gallery this afternoon.'

With monumental reluctance, they pulled apart and rearranged their clothing. Olympia sighed inwardly as she looked at Joachim's gorgeous, youthful body. If only there was time. But a would-be Légionnaire must never be diverted from the one true purpose, however delicious the diversion might be.

'Shall I come with you to the Galérie? He might try to harm you.' Joachim did up his belt and picked up his denim jacket from the floor.

'I . . . no. It's very gallant of you, sweetheart, but best if you don't.' She realised that she had already risked disaster by telling him as much as she had. If she revealed the whole truth about her quest to join the Légion, she could lose everything, and maybe even put Joachim in danger. She turned to him and kissed him on the cheek. 'I'll be fine.'

Joachim looked doubtful. 'Promise?'

'Promise. Now, how about getting me out of here before somebody realises what's been going on?'

'No problem.'

Joachim pushed open the door of the cubicle, only to be confronted by two teenage punks, in an obvious state of excitement. One was rubbing the crotch of his filthy ripped jeans, and their intentions were not difficult to divine.

'Nice show,' observed one of the boys, unzipping his jeans.

'*Pas mal*,' agreed his companion. 'She's a bit of all right, your bird. Got some to spare for us too, darlin'?' He reached out and squeezed Olympia's breasts, so hard that she winced. 'Nice an' firm. Bet she's got a lovely tight one, haven't you darlin'?'

Enraged, Joachim launched himself forward and

punched the green-haired punk. His fist landed on the boy's jaw with a satisfying crunch, but in a moment his companion was on Joachim's back, wrenching back his head so that his green-haired partner in crime could get a good swing at it.

'*Assez!*' Olympia was seriously angry now, but no one was paying her much attention. 'That is quite enough!'

She blessed the day Lymhurst College had asked the local crime prevention unit to run self-defence classes for all the senior pupils. An arm-lock, followed by a swift kick to the chin, sent the green-haired punk spinning across the floor of the toilets. He landed up against the back wall with a thud, and lay where he fell, an expression of utter disbelief on his spotty adolescent face.

'For goodness' sake come *on*, Joachim!' urged Olympia. 'Before someone hears and comes to see what's going on. She dragged him off the second punk, who was shielding his face with his puny white arms as Joachim rained blows on him like a human whirlwind.

They left the two punks breathless and dizzy on the toilet floor, and slipped out through the door back into the museum. No one paid them the slightest attention as they strolled arm in arm through the galleries and out through the main entrance.

Olympia left Joachim outside the glass pyramid of the Grand Louvre, and set out on foot for the Galérie Sainte Marie. The afternoon sun was blazing hot on her back, and sent a little trickle of sweat running down between her shoulder-blades. She thought how nice it would be to have Joachim there with her, to lick it away. And how nice to be able to lick the sweat from his smooth, golden body.

There it was. The Galérie Sainte Marie. Would the porcelain figures be there, acting out their eternal tableau, or would Monsignor Testi have reneged on their little bargain? Everything rested on her success – if she failed now, she would have let down the Légion completely. The dream would be gone forever.

She stood in front of the shop window, hardly daring to open her eyes and look. She scanned the display quickly, and her heart sank. No sign of the porcelain group; and no label reading 'The Triumph of Venus'.

And then she saw it. A group of three exquisitely crafted porcelain figures, at the side of the window, and almost at the back. The man's eyes were closed in an expession of perpetual, frozen ecstasy as he buried his face in the blonde girl's love-lips and a triumphant Venus brought down the cruel lash upon his martyred back. Olympia had to laugh as she read the label in front of it. It read:

'The Consequences of Lust'.

The next morning, the messenger arrived a little earlier than usual, and knocked on the door of Olympia's room.

'Entrez.'

He pushed open the door and walked in, to find the room apparently deserted.

'I'm in here,' called Olympia from the bathroom.

'Oh, I . . . er . . . would you prefer it if I waited outside?'

Olympia exploded in gales of laughter.

'Don't be such a prat. After what happened the other day, do you really think we've still got any secrets from each other? For heaven's sake, come in.'

Olympia was wallowing in a rather delicious honeysuckle-scented bath, surrounded by bubbles but with just the right amount of naked flesh on view to provoke palpitations in any passing male. The effect was not lost on the messenger, who became so painfully erect that he had to adjust himself surreptitiously when Olympia turned to put down the soap.

'Have some Lanson, *chérie*.' Olympia indicated a champagne bottle in an ice-bucket at the side of the bath. 'It's properly chilled, and there's some caviar left if you're hungry.'

'Well, it's a little early, but, why not?' The messenger helped himself to a glass of champagne and a biscuit with a little heap of caviar on the top. 'What are you celebrating, by the way?'

'Do I have to be celebrating anything?' retorted Olympia. 'I just adore champagne and caviar, and besides, I did think I managed rather well with Monsignor Testi.'

'Not to mention the two punks in the gentlemen's lavatories at the Grand Louvre,' muttered the messenger, biting into his biscuit. 'You know, enthusiasm is all very laudable in a prospective Légionnaire, but you really ought to be more careful. You could come to real harm.'

'I know how to handle myself,' replied Olympia. 'Leading the life I do, it's essential. I pride myself on my independence, so I have to provide for the consequences.' She sipped champagne, and stretched out luxuriously in the bath. 'Anyhow, what's a terribly nice boy like you doing in the Légion d'Amour? Surely you're far too much of a gentleman!'

The messenger shook his head.

'I'm sorry, Olympia, but I cannot tell you anything about the Légion unless and until you are admitted to its ranks. And if I were you,' he added, 'I'd learn to be more discreet. That boyfriend of yours . . . Lavallier, is it? Well, you really shouldn't have enlisted his help in the last task.'

'I didn't tell him much. Aren't I even allowed a teensy-weensy little cheat?' pouted Olympia in mock resentment.

The messenger grew silent and serious.

'Look, Olympia.' He ran an appreciate finger underneath the bath foam and over the ample curve of her breast, making her shiver with enjoyment. 'You're a worthy candidate, but you just don't seem to understand the dangers you are in. You're playing with fire! Didn't your father ever explain?'

'He explained how much the Légion meant to him; how desperately he longed to become a member.'

'But surely . . . Olympia, the Légion is utterly ruthless against those who threaten it, you must understand that. The penalty for failure, as you know, is exile; but the penalty for betrayal . . .'

Olympia's eyes widened in alarm. For the first time, she was beginning to feel a twinge of real unease.

'What are you saying?'

'I am saying, Olympia, that if you value your life, you will do nothing to endanger the secrecy and integrity of the Légion d'Amour. You would do well to remember my words, and not take these challenges quite so lightly.'

He drank down the last of the champagne, and set down the glass on the floor. Then he produced an envelope from his briefcase.

'Are you ready for today's task, my dear?'

Olympia accepted the envelope and tore it open, half-afraid of what it might contain. Inside was a silver card; the message was longer than the previous ones, but simple enough.

Congratulations on your success thus far, Olympia Deschamps. You have succeeded beyond our expectations, and you are a credit to your late father's memory.

Your task today is one of service. Tonight, at eight o'clock, a stranger will come to your room. Others will follow – one each hour for the next ten hours. You must satisfy all of them, no matter how bizarre or extreme their demands. If you do not, you will be deemed to have failed the trials.

'You have all day today to prepare for the trial,' said the messenger. 'Use it well. There is an arduous night ahead of you. At all costs, do not exhaust your sexual energies. I would strongly advise abstaining from all sexual activity until this evening.'

'Don't worry – I will do it,' replied Olympia, determinedly. 'Whatever it takes, I will succeed.'

Olympia sat in her room for a while after the messenger had gone, musing over what he had said. How could she prepare for what lay ahead of her? Should she rest; or should she get out and do some work, to take her mind off the night's tasks? The idea of a whole day without sex held little appeal, but if it was really necessary to her success . . .

Inevitably her hand strayed once more to her father's battered old diary, and eagerly she unlocked it, hopeful of finding some inspiration. She opened it at one of the later pages, and read what he had written, all those years ago.

Wednesday, 8 April. Today I waited for many hours but no message came. I went as instructed to the Café Al Akhim, but no one came to instruct me. I concluded, therefore, that I had been deemed to have failed the trials, and that the Légion had not even bothered to tell me of my failure.

In despair, I decided to return to the Pension Lautréamont, but on my way back through the narrow side-streets, I was accosted by an old Arab woman, heavily veiled, who told me that she had 'many beautiful daughters'. In my state of disappointment, I scarcely thought of fleshly stimulation, but she was so insistent that in the end I agreed to go with her into her house of pleasure, believing that I now had nothing left to lose.

Entering through a beaded curtain, I discovered myself in the most perfect representation of an Eastern harem. The walls were richly draped with brightly-coloured tapestries, and the rooms divided by intricately carved screens, which both veiled and enhanced the beauties of the women within. For, to my immense surprise, they were indeed beautiful. Suddenly I

167

realised that I was at the mercy of twelve raven-haired beauties with flashing eyes, all intent on pleasure.

'My daughters are hungry for love,' the old woman told me. 'Their husband is far away, and they burn for the love of a strong and virile young man.' She ran her hands over me, as though testing my flesh for firmness; and even slid her fingers over my groin, feeling my manhood beginning to swell at the sight of so much barely-veiled flesh. 'It is well,' she announced to her 'daughters'. 'You may take your pleasure of him.'

If I had imagined that this was a simple bordello, and that I would be free to explore the delights of the house as I pleased, I was shortly to be very surprised indeed. For the 'daughters' of the house were voracious, sex-hungry women who fell upon me like vampires thirsty for blood. They tore at my clothing, eager to run their hands over my body, tasting my flesh with their tongues, cupping my testicles in their cool, cool hands until I could have wept for pleasure.

Such was their insistence that I was obliged to pleasure each of them in turn, following their bidding until all declared themselves satisfied and I was exhausted and weak. They made me kiss each one of them to ecstasy, withholding my own satisfaction until they were each hungry to be pleasured a second time.

When at last they had finished with me, I turned to the old woman, thinking that I should now be allowed to put on my clothes and leave. Imagine my surprise and horror when I turned round and saw a huge negro with a scimitar, guarding the only door out of the house.

'Madam!' I cried. 'If it is money you wish for, I shall be happy to pay whatever price. For I have enjoyed some small pleasure in your bordello.'

But the old woman gave a horrible laugh.

'This is no house of ill-repute,' she told me. 'It is the harem of Sultan Ab-el-Raschid. These are his wives; and if he finds out that you have been taking your pleasure with them in his absence, his rage will know no bounds. I am the Sultan's mother. He will believe anything I choose to tell him. Abdul here is the jealous protector of his master's interest. Would you like me to hand you over to him?'

'No!' I cried. 'But what am I do to?'

'The answer is a simple one,' she replied. And as I looked into her veiled face, her eyes glittered small and black, like a lizard's. 'You must pleasure me – or die. The choice is yours.'

Faced with this unpalatable choice I knew what I must do; and there and then, on the richly carpeted floor of the Sultan's harem, I made passionate love to the hideous, withered old woman who so craved my body. She drained me of every ounce of energy I had left, but at last, when I feared I could do no more, she showed me a glimmer of mercy.

'You are a worth adversary, infidel,' she told me as she veiled herself once more from my eyes. 'And because you have pleasured me and all my beautiful daughters-in-law, I shall soften my heart to you. You may leave this house alive.

'But mark my words. Five minutes after you

have left, Abdul will pursue you into the streets of this city. If he finds you, he will kill you, as is his right. For have you not sullied the honour of the Sultan's wives and of his mother also?'

I was speechless with horror and outrage, but what could I do? I took to my heels and ran through the back-streets as fast as my legs would carry me, at every moment believing I heard the pounding of Abdul's footsteps, the swish of his scimitar as he pursued me to exact his master's vengeance.

When at last I reached the relative safety of the Pension Lautréamont, I found a visitor waiting for me in my room. It was the messenger I had waited for in vain at the Café Al Akhim.

'Congratulations, Monsieur,' he said. 'You have passed the fifth trial.'

Olympia closed the diary and sat for a moment in silence, wondering what the night would hold in store for her. Would she ever match up to her father's resourcefulness and skill? Would there be dangers in store for her, too?

She stretched out lazily on the bed, listening to the sounds of city life in the street below. 'Rest,' the messenger had said. 'Save yourself, and prepare for what lies ahead.' But what should she do? She was in the mood for fun, and yet if she indulged her sensual whims, she might have no energy left for the night's ordeals.

Perhaps work was the answer, after all. There were all those galleries she really ought to visit in the Quartier Latin; and afterwards, she could treat herself to a little visit to Joachim's studio. Strictly to talk business, of course.

At that moment, the phone on the bedside table trilled into life, jolting Olympia back from her sensual reveries. She picked up the receiver.

'*Allô?*'

'Olympia, darling! It's been simply ages!'

'Caroline? What on earth are you doing in Paris?'

'The orchestra's doing a European tour, and whilst we're playing Paris, I'm trying to strike a sponsorship deal with some ghastly industrialist who fancies himself as an impresario. It's all terribly boring, darling. I'm simply longing for some time off.'

'Why don't we get together for coffee?' suggested Olympia, recalling Caroline's legendary capacity for alcohol. She didn't want to face the coming night with a hangover.

'Oh, I've got a much better idea,' replied Caroline, brightly. 'My boss has given me the whole day off. Why don't we spend all of it together, a girls' day out, like when we were at Harries and Theakston?'

Olympia winced. Normally, she would be only too glad to spend a day with her old chum Caroline, but the memory of their early days together in publishing sounded alarm bells deep inside her head.

'Well, I'm a bit busy,' she said doubtfully, desperately searching for excuses to defer their meeting.

'Nonsense!' retorted Caroline. 'You work far too hard. Always did. I'm sure it's nothing that can't wait until tomorrow. I'll be waiting for you in the hotel lobby in half an hour. And be sure you dress up to the nines – I fancy my chances with all these gorgeous French hunks!'

As Olympia replaced the receiver, she couldn't suppress an affectionate chuckle as she remembered all the scandalous things they'd got up to together at Harries and Theakston.

Caroline DeVere and Olympia Deschamps had joined the renowned fine art publishers together, straight from one of those intensive ten-week secretarial courses at a finishing school for nicely bred young ladies. From their first day at the publishing house, Olympia knew that Caroline was a girl after her own heart. She barged into the chief designer's office one lunchtime, to discover Caroline taking down more than her boss's dictation; and from that day on they had become inseparable friends.

She smiled as she remembered the launch party for *The Sensual Art of Ancient Egypt*, which Caroline had organised. It was a terribly lavish affair, held – at massive expense – in the Egyptian Gallery of the British Museum, and the drinks and canapés were served by pretty boys and girls in authentic Egyptian costume.

Their diaphanous clothing was enough to turn anyone's head, and after a few glasses of free champagne, the author became rather inebriated and made a play for one of the boys. Disaster! One of Fleet Street's finest tabloid lensmen was on hand to immortalise the very moment when Frederick Courtney invited a blushing boy to unzip his bulging flies.

Caroline had to act quickly. After all, it wasn't just Courtney's reputation that was at stake. She had the good of the entire publishing house to think of. No one else seemed to know what to do, so she did what came naturally and set about seducing the photographer.

Finding an excuse for a private conversation, Caroline led the pressman through the gallery of a secluded alcove behind an exhibition of sacred jewellery and tomb furnishings. Intrigued, Olympia followed at a discreet distance, and hid behind a display cabinet.

In the alcove, Caroline was wasting no time. Seasoned hack though he was, the photographer was far from immune to Caroline's considerable charms; and the champagne was doing its work on him, too. He grinned inanely as Caroline pressed him up against an enormous statue of Tuthmosis III, her massive, pneumatic breasts pressing into his chest and her taut belly grinding hard up against his pelvis.

'You're a very handsome man, do you know that?'

Olympia could almost have believed that she meant it as she listened to Caroline purring in the man's ear, her fingers running all over his sweaty body. Caroline sure was a smooth operator.

'You're . . . not so bad yourself.' The pressman had leered and made a grab for Caroline's left breast, squeezing it with more enthusiasm than finesse.

'Do you know what I think? I think you're wasted on this crummy job,' purred Caroline, as she flattered her victim into a false sense of security. 'I've always admired your work, you know.'

'Really?'

'Oh yes.' She had let her fingers skim his crotch, titillating but not satisfying the need for touch. He gave a groan, closed his eyes and leant back against the smooth stone.

'You should be in art photography.' She undid

the buttons of his shirt, and planted wet kisses on his chest. 'I could help you get on in this business, you know. I know people. My uncle's the Duke of Flamborough.'

As Olympia watched her friend's skilful seduction technique, she had begun to feel desire warming her belly; and surreptitiously slipped a hand up underneath her skirt and inside her knickers. She was hot, moist and ready; and her own touch on her clitoris felt deliciously electric.

'And why should a classy bird like you want to help me, eh?' The photographer opened a cynical eye and surveyed his seductress, evidently battling manfully to resist the temptations of the flesh. His camera was still dangling from its strap around his wrist; he wasn't going to let go of a scoop that easily.

'Because I fancy you something rotten, that's why.' Caroline had unfastened the photographer's belt with agonising slowness. 'Have you never heard of girls liking a bit of rough?'

He laughed and clutched at her backside, pulling up her tight skirt to expose the black satin cami-knickers which Caroline always wore.

'If you don't believe me, why don't you feel? Go on, feel how much I want you.'

Far from reluctant to oblige, the photographer slid a fat finger under the hem of the loose cami-knickers, and into the steamy jungle between Caroline's thighs. She gave a little sigh as he touched her, not without skill, and ran his fingers along her moist furrow.

'Hot and wet,' he murmured. 'Just how I like my women.'

She tugged down the zipper and thrust a hand into his pants, making him shudder with pleasure.

'Hot and hard,' she smiled. 'And that's just how I like my men.'

In a moment they were kissing passionately, mouths crushed together, tongues jousting in a turmoil of lust; and Olympia saw that Caroline's lust was getting the better of her. Would she forget her greater purpose in her pursuit of the transient sexual high?

The photographer edged a little to the side, and sat down on a convenient smaller statue of the Pharaoh Ramses II, who would no doubt have been quite surprised to find two lovers embracing on his lap.

He pulled out his manhood and invited Caroline to sit on him. In a moment they were moving together in silent, synchronized rhythm; and Olympia could see from the blissful expression on Caroline's face that she was enjoying the experience as much as the photographer was. He was biting her neck, gently but insistently, and she was arching her back in pleasure as she rode him in slow-motion ecstasy.

At the moment of crisis, the photographer opened his mouth in a silent cry; and his grip on the camera strap loosened, for just a second. But in that second, Caroline had seized the camera from him and wrenched open the back, exposing the film.

It was a legendary *tour-de-force*. The outraged photographer got the sack; Caroline got promotion; and Olympia had enjoyed a delicious night of passion with a rather hunky art dealer who later took her on as a trainee in his Bond Street gallery.

And now here she was, a successful art dealer, in Paris to enjoy the latest talent in more ways than one. Caroline's career had been a meteoric one, too. Within a few years, her remarkable initiative – and her ability to drink any man under the Boardroom table – had taken her into PR, and the latest Olympia had heard, Caroline was the marketing manager for an internationally-renowned philharmonic orchestra.

Well, she mustn't let Caroline lead her into bad ways this time. There was too much at stake. For once in her life, Olympia Deschamps must strive to be the soul of abstinence. She could only hope that Caroline would understand. With a sigh, she picked up her handbag and went down to meet her friend.

She found Caroline rather elegantly sprawled across an eighteenth-century chaise longue in the hotel lobby, flirting outrageously with an admiring male on either side. She was even more flamboyant, even more glamorous, even more blonde than Olympia remembered her, with that sure fashion sense that allowed her always to remain just on the right side of bad taste. When she saw Olympia, she leapt to her feet and embraced her with a squeal of delight.

'You're here, at last! It's been so long! How long is it . . . two years now?'

'At the Metropole Hotel, in Brighton. Do you remember that sales conference?'

Caroline giggled with the wicked remembrance.

'Gosh he was gorgeous. I ran off with him to the Côte D'Azur for five weeks, did I ever tell you?'

176

Olympia shook her head.

'He was wonderful in bed, you know – hung like a horse, and virile with it. But he was so bloody boring! All he ever talked about was "maximising his capital outlay".'

'So what did you do?'

'I left him at the Hôtel Mirabelle in Nice, and took off for Los Angeles with a billionaire property tycoon. It did wonders for my career. In the six months I spent in LA, I met Xavier, and that's how I ended up working for the orchestra. But that's enough about me. You're still in the same job, then? Your friend Chris at the gallery told me where you were staying.'

'I'm a full partner in the gallery now. Signing Mikhail Alexikov last year did a lot for my reputation.'

'So this is a business trip, then?'

'Not . . . entirely.'

'So we can have some fun together, then? Just like the old days?'

'Well, no. I'm sort of . . . er . . . celibate at the moment.'

'What!' Caroline spluttered into her gin and tonic. 'You – celibate? This is some sort of joke, isn't it?'

'It's all meant to increase the power of my sexual experiences,' explained Olympia indignantly, hoping that she sounded convincing. 'Every now and then I abstain for a while, to heighten my sexual desire.'

'Oh.' Caroline looked disappointed. 'So no bonking then?'

'Not today. But we can still have fun.'

Caroline brightened.

'Of course we can. Now, get your things and let's go. I've booked us lunch on a bâteau mouche. Carlos – he's the solo cellist – tells me they do a wonderful brioche aux champignons.'

They set off for the river, and as they walked Olympia began to relax. The trials seemed very far away as they strolled together in the warm July sunshine. Maybe she was overreacting, and she could afford to let herself have a little fun.

The boat was moored under the bridge at Alma Marceau, and just preparing to cast off. So they boarded hurriedly, stumbling down five or six highly-polished steps into the saloon, where lunch was to be served. A rather sexy waiter slid his hand over Olympia's backside as he helped her down the steps, and she felt a sudden pang of hunger that had nothing to do with brioche aux champignons.

As Olympia had feared, Caroline started drinking immediately and showed no signs of slowing down, even by the time they got to the third course. Olympia stuck to mineral water mixed with a little white wine, and spent most of the time observing her fellow diners. A group of rich Americans talked and chewed noisily as the boat glided slowly downriver, paying not the slightest attention to the scenery. By way of contrast, a gaggle of Japanese businessmen, all in identical blue suits, snapped away at anything and everything, probably without the faintest idea of what they were taking pictures of. Meanwhile Caroline, who had seemed so very keen to chat about old times with her dear friend Olympia, was knocking back double cognacs and flirting with the wine waiter.

Rather bored by all of this, Olympia considered going up on deck to get away from the noisy Americans and the snap-happy Japanese. But then something rather entertaining happened.

'*Zut alors!* I have dropped my knife.' Olympia looked up to see that the distinctly handsome young businessman sitting opposite her was regarding the floor with exaggerated horror. Was this little pantomime all for her benefit, she wondered.

'Why don't you pick it up?' she suggested helpfully.

'Why not, indeed?' The young man flashed her a smile. Then he slipped down off his seat and disappeared under the table. A few seconds later, Olympia felt something brush against her knees. She thought nothing of it until the contact was repeated; this time with much deliberation.

She tried shifting away, but hands held her legs fast.

'Don't be alarmed,' a voice whispered from underneath the table. 'I wish only to pleasure you.'

Olympia groaned inwardly, yearning for pleasure yet knowing that she ought to resist, for the sake of the trials. He was handsome. He was desirable. He wanted her and she wanted him. Already she could imagine the blissful warmth of his tongue, exploring the yielding flesh between her thighs; running gently over her mound of pleasure until at last it penetrated the very depths of her, opening the floodgates of desire.

With a determined gesture, she wrenched her legs apart.

'Leave me alone,' she hissed.

The hands left her, and she heard the young

man scrambling about under the table. A moment later, he emerged, red-faced and tousled. He straightened his tie, picked up his knife and resumed his lunch.

'*Pardon, Mademoiselle,*' he said coldly. 'I had thought you were a woman of passion. Clearly I was wrong.'

His words cut to the quick. Glancing around for reassurance, Olympia saw that Caroline had disappeared. Maybe the combination of too much alcohol and the oppressive noonday heat had finally got to her, after all, and she'd gone up on deck for some fresh air? Olympia pushed back her chair. If Caroline was throwing up over the side, she was going to need someone to moan at.

She pushed past the other diners and climbed up the short flight of steps to the deck. It seemed deserted, except for the lone man steering the boat along the river. He winked as Olympia passed, but she paid him no attention.

She stood on deck for a little while, watching the sights drift slowly past, then walked round to the stern to see if Caroline was there. As she rounded the cabin, she stopped dead in her tracks.

Caroline was indeed on deck. She might be drunk, but she certainly wasn't ill. She was leaning forwards over the rail, laughing hysterically as the hunky waiter – the very same one who had seemed so taken with Olympia's backside – made passionate love to her. His strong, muscular hands were cupping her breasts, and he was thrusting into her from behind, with a smooth, regular rhythm. Anyone watching from the bank might think they were just two affectionate lovers, embracing closely as they stood on deck to watch the sights.

But standing directly behind them, Olympia had the full benefit of their joyous lovemaking, and could not suppress a surge of excitement.

Her footsteps on the deck must have disturbed them, for the waiter glanced over his shoulder at her and grinned.

'Why do you not join us, Mademoiselle? Your friend is a very good lover, but I am hungry for you also.'

Olympia was desperately tempted. He was so handsome, so exciting. Even his arrogant approach aroused her. She looked him up and down, taking in the tight backside, the broad shoulders, the golden hair framing the tanned face; and she wanted him so badly. Wanted to feel his arms about her, his hands caressing her breasts. Wanted him to make passionate love to her, as he was doing to her friend Caroline, who was thrusting out her bottom for him like an eager mare.

'Some other time, perhaps,' she said regretfully, turning away and walking back towards the companionway.

Caroline reappeared in the saloon about half an hour later, cheeks flushed and eyes sparkling. The boat was gliding slowly towards its moorings.

'Had a good time?' enquired Olympia, archly.

'Oh, don't be like that, Olympia. It's not my fault if you're depriving yourself of the finer things in life.' She took a powder compact out of her handbag, and checked her make-up. 'Besides, Bernard's such a sweetie.' She giggled. 'In fact, I'm seeing him again tonight. Now then, what shall we do next? We really must find you some fun.'

'How about shopping? Or an art gallery?' sug-

gested Olympia feebly. She couldn't risk any more
of Caroline's little pranks.

Caroline pulled a face.

'I said fun, darling!' She thought for a moment.
'I know! How about a nice, relaxing massage, to
ease away all those terrible tensions and frus-
trations, you've been inflicting on yourself? You
always did enjoy massage, didn't you?'

'What sort of massage?' demanded Olympia,
suspiciously.

'Oriental Shia-tsu – it's all perfectly innocent, I
can assure you. I know an absolute darling of a
masseur.'

'Well, I suppose it will be all right.'

And so it was that Caroline and Olympia set off
for a small and very exclusive health club in the
XVIᵉ arrondissement.

The Club Jacinthe was like a sparkling oasis of
tranquility amid the heat and bustle of city life.

'I always come here to be pampered when I'm
in Paris,' explained Caroline as they came out of
the sauna. 'It's so delightful, having all one's needs
catered for.' She grinned. 'And a day here does
wonders for the sex drive, I can tell you. You can
forget all that celibacy nonsense. Now, how about
that massage?'

'Lovely,' sighed Olympia, relaxed and happy.

'Well, you just wait there. I'm off for a swim.
See you later, in the bar.'

Olympia stretched out on the massage table,
face-down under a fluffy white towel. Life was
good. She felt so relaxed, yet so alive, as though
her body had been awakened from a long sleep.
She must have dozed for a few minutes, because

she was awakened from her reverie by a soft oriental voice.

'Mademoiselle Deschamps?'

She opened her eyes and turned her head to one side. There, standing beside the massage bed, was a tall, middle-aged Japanese man, dressed in a plain white robe belted at the waist.

'I didn't expect a man!'

'You need have no fear, Mademoiselle. I am entirely at your disposal, to command as you desire. I work only by touch, for as you will see, I am entirely blind.'

She realised with a start that he was staring glassily at her, the black diamonds of his eyes blank and unseeing. She remembered the blind man on the train, and it suddenly occurred to her that she had never seen the eyes behind those dark glasses. Did they also have this expressionless brilliance, this dark mystery?

'If you will allow me, Mademoiselle, I shall begin by removing your towel.'

She relaxed swiftly under his skilful touch. His fingers were like butterfly wings, incredibly light and forever moving, stroking, fluttering over her flesh.

'There is tension here, and here.' He exerted gentle pressure on the muscles around her shoulder-blades, and she was surprised to feel a dull, deep pain. 'You are under much stress at the moment, I think.'

'A little,' confessed Olympia.

'I will soothe it away for you,' promised the masseur, feeling his way around her body with the soft touch of an angel, easing the tension out of her muscles and joints. Olympia luxuriated

183

under his hands, finding his touch increasingly pleasurable, his voice somehow erotic. There was a heady, musky fragrance in the room, and Olympia wondered vaguely if he was burning aphrodisiac herbs and spices. With each breath she took, she seemed to grow more relaxed and yet more excited.

'If you will please to turn on to your back now, Mademoiselle.'

She rolled over, unafraid to bare her body in the presence of this sightless healer, whose hands moved with a smooth, hypnotic motion that both soothed and excited. His fingers began at her shoulders, loosening them with a broad, circular motion; then working their way down her flanks, gently kneading. A few drops of a warm, sweetly-fragrant oil made her shiver with pleasure, and he worked the oil into her belly, the tops of her thighs.

'You are a beautiful woman, Mademoiselle. Your skin is as smooth and soft as a child's.'

She sighed with delight, hardly realising that slowly, so slowly, he was working his way closer to the heart of her sex.

'Let me relax you, Mademoiselle. Let me soothe your tensions away.'

'I . . . don't know,' gasped Olympia, responding to his touch in spite of herself. 'I shouldn't.'

'Relax, and I will give you pleasure. Pleasure greater than you have ever dreamed.'

His hands slid from the top of her thighs to her lower belly, skimming her pubis and brushing against the entrance to her sex. Then he slid a finger between her love-lips.

Olympia cried out as his fingertip entered the

184

heart of her. She must resist, as she had sworn to
herself. She must not give in to pleasure.

'Relax,' the voice commanded her; and she felt
her strength ebbing away. 'Relax, and let me
worship the beauty of your body.'

All her reistance gone now, she felt her thighs
open to welcome in the masseur's knowing hands.
Her whole body was now solely the vessel of
pleasure. Every nerve-ending was screaming for
release. Her anxiety had been replaced by a very
different tension: the tension of expectation. The
tension of a heavy sky before the storm breaks.

'Mercy . . .' she gasped, her fingernails digging
into the backs of the masseur's hand as she felt
pleasure lapping at her like a crystal-clear, tropical
ocean. 'You don't understand. You mustn't . . .' But
he was not listening. He was quietly carrying out
his work, massaging her to a peak of purest delight.

'Free yourself, child. Let pleasure be your
guide.'

'No. I cannot. I must not.'

'Accept the freedom of pleasure. More pleasure
yet awaits.'

With a long sigh, she fell back on to the couch.
Ecstasy washed over her and she abandoned herself to the inexorable tide. As the delicious spasms
ebbed away, the masseur's voice was warm and
subtle in her ears.

'Have no fear, child. There will be more
pleasure, and yet more.'

She opened her eyes and looked at him
quizzically.

'What do you mean?'

He felt in the pocket of his robe and handed her
a small vial.

185

'In this bottle lies the secret blend of oils with which I coaxed you to pleasure, Mademoiselle. Tell me, is there a warmth, an excitement still in your belly?'

'Yes; yes, there is. Like a delicious burning.'

'The sensations of desire will not leave you, Mademoiselle, if you continue to anoint yourself with this oil. It stimulates the pleasure-receptors in the skin and mucous membranes. As long as you continue to rub it into your body, your desires will grow. No one can resist its gentle power.'

'Thank you,' said Olympia, gazing at the tiny bottle in her hands. Could a simple blend of oils really be so powerful?

'But beware,' the masseur warned her. 'Do not use too much. If you do, your appetite may become a terrible, uncontrollable hunger.'

That evening, Caroline went off for dinner – and bed – with Bernard, and Olympia dined alone at the hotel, then returned to her room to prepare herself. Thoughts of what was to become of her spun round and round in her mind as she bathed, rubbed a few drops of the oil into her skin and dressed in a black bustier and tight lycra skirt. As an afterthought, she trickled a few more drops on to the palm of her hand, and used the fragrant oil to anoint her belly and thighs. Instantly a familiar warmth began to spread over her.

There was a knock on the door. Olympia glanced at the clock on the bedside table. Ten o'clock, just as the messenger had said.

'Fair enough,' she smiled to herself as she walked over to open the door. 'I'm ready for you now, whoever you are.'

Chapter Nine

'*Bonsoir, Mademoiselle.*'
The man was tall, good-looking in a cynical sort of way, and smartly dressed in a well-tailored grey suit and hand-finished shirt. There was an air of slight seediness about him; a laziness that hinted at the truth of his existence. This was a man who did not work for his money. Olympia looked him up and down, and wondered just how many elderly, rich old women's beds he had sweet-talked his way into. Yes, this was a man for whom women's pleasure was a very lucrative business.

Now, it seemed, Olympia must attend to his pleasure.

She ushered him in silently, unsure of what to do or say. He flashed her a half-smile, and she thought to herself that maybe this would not be so difficult after all. He was a man after all, and she never had any difficulty in understanding men's needs.

'Drink?'

'A dry Martini, if you have one.'

As she poured the vermouth her hand trembled slightly, making the neck of the bottle chink against the side of the glass. A glance at the clock showed that time was ticking by. She didn't want to rush things, but this visitor was to be the first of many, and the conversation must soon turn to sex.

She handed him the Martini. He took a small sip, then yawned and stretched, looking her up and down with an expression of bored amusement.

'I suppose you think I'm going to make the first move.'

Olympia was rather taken aback.

'What makes you say that?'

'Well, if you do, you can think again. Believe me, I've seen it all, done it all, had 'em all, too: fat women, thin women, old women – even the occasional beautiful young woman, like you. But it's all the same to me, you see. Nothing excites me any more.'

'I see.'

Olympia was pulling off her tight black skirt, rolling it down over her taut, golden thighs.

'A brave try, *chérie*,' he smiled. 'But really, do you seriously think I've never seen a pretty girl naked before? Do you honestly think you can show me anything new?'

Perhaps not show, thought Olympia grimly, but there's a chance that I can make you feel something very new.

She crossed to the dressing table, picked up the little vial of oil that the Japanese masseur had given her, and unscrewed the dropper.

'Perhaps you'd like me to massage you? My lovers tell me I'm quite skilful.'

'A massage? With oil? Oh, how quaint.' He yawned and glanced at his watch. 'Still, I suppose it will pass the time. *D'accord*, why not?'

He took off his jacket and allowed Olympia to help him out of his rather elegant cashmere trousers, which she folded neatly on the back of a chair. He was wearing boxer shorts in rose-pink silk, which she thought rather absurd; but his body was in the peak of condition for a man of his middle years – nice and firm, with an appealing ripple of muscle beneath the deeply tanned skin.

'Perhaps you'd like to lie down on the bed?'

He stretched out, belly down, on the satin sheets, clearly not expecting to derive much enjoyment from the experience. Well, she would see about that. Olympia rolled the bottle of oil in her hands, warming the priceless liquid, then let a few drops fall on to his golden back. What if it didn't work on him? What if its effects on her had all been the result of auto-suggestion?

'Mmm. Smells quite pleasant,' he murmured grudgingly as she set to work on him. 'Sort of sweetish – no, spicy, musky. What's in it?'

Olympia did not reply, but continued rubbing his flesh as the masseur had done to her, making sure to massage the blended oils deeply into his skin. Little by little, he began to relax under her hands, and his breathing quickened. Olympia realised with delight that the powerful aphrodisiacs in the oil must be starting to take effect.

'Mmm,' he murmured. 'Feels nice. Warm . . . so very warm.'

Sensing him grow more receptive to her touch,

she rolled him over on to his back, and put a few drops of the oil in the palm of her hand. His pleasure was beginning to manifest itself. Good. But there was still some resistance to break down. She ran her hands over his chest and belly, paying particular attention to the pinkish crests of his nipples, which were showing signs of responding to her touch.

His thighs parted obligingly to admit her tremulous hands, but she did not immediately touch his penis, by now semi-erect and moistening at the tip. Better to tease him first, make him really hungry for her. As the first drop of oil trickled over his scrotum, a gasp of astonishment escaped from his lips.

'*Diable! Qu'est-ce que* . . .? What fires of Hell . . .? *Ah, Mon Dieu, que le plaisir est exquis!* You have the Devil in your fingertips, Mademoiselle.'

Olympia smiled to herself, certain now that she had this man's pleasure in the palm of her hand – literally. He began groaning as she massaged the oil deeper and deeper into his velvety sac with long, slow, luxurious strokes.

The effect was almost instantaneous, and when she next touched the excited flesh of his shaft, it was like an iron rod in her fist.

'Make me come now,' he moaned. 'My cock feels as if it's on fire.'

At last Olympia had him where she wanted him. She knew she could bring him to climax in a few strokes of her hand, if she chose to. But no: she wanted his pleasure to be more memorable than that.

'Never forget this moment, Monsieur,' she whispered as she climbed astride him and his hardness slid into the very depths of her. 'Never forget Olympia Deschamps.'

The young Arab boy hovered on the threshold of the hotel room, unsure whether to be excited or embarrassed. The man who had accosted him in the street had offered him pleasure; the pleasure of a woman's body for the first time in his young life – and money, too, lots of it. But as he stood in the doorway and looked at the half-naked beauty with the flashing emerald eyes and red-gold hair, he felt half-inclined to turn tail and run.

'*Entrez, entrez*. Don't be so afraid. I won't eat you.'

But then again, maybe I will, thought Olympia as she pushed the boy gently into the room and closed the door behind him. He *was* a delicious little sweetmeat, after all: barely sixteen, and as wide-eyed and nervous as a startled fawn.

'What . . . what do you want me to do, Madame?'

'Nothing, *mon cher*. Nothing at all. I shall take care of everything. My only wish is to give you pleasure. And please don't call me "Madame" – it makes me feel so old! You can call me Olympia.

'Now, why don't you take off some of these clothes? It's such a hot night, and you'd be so much more comfortable without them.'

He flinched as she laid hands upon him, almost as if he feared she was about to hurt him in some way. This little street urchin was not accustomed to gentleness. She began talking nonsense to him; soothing him as though he were a tiny child, or a baby wild animal frightened at being parted from its mother. A little tiger-cub, that's what he was.

Strength and softness and fierce hunger, all combined in this sublimely beautiful form.

'*Cher p'tit tigre*,' she purred, stripping off his T-shirt and undoing the button on his jeans.

He began murmuring in a gutteral dialect peppered with expressions she did not understand – an Arab-French patois, she supposed – and Olympia imagined he was talking to her in the language of the jungle beasts. He was so exotic, so wild, so delectable. She ran her fingers through his mop of curly brown hair, and sure enough, he growled with a pleasure that was tinged with the piquant taste of fear.

As she stripped off his jeans, she saw that he was already massively, painfully erect, and the tip of his penis was weeping moisture on to his white cotton pants. She longed to lick away these tears of love; but she did not want to risk terrifying him or driving him away.

Very gently, she laid her hand on the waistband of the boy's pants and pulled them down, exposing the lively shaft beneath.

'Beautiful little tiger cub,' she growled. 'Let me kiss you, caress you.'

But as she touched him, his youthful inexperience took over and a white-hot love jet fountained out of him. He cried out with shame and distress, hiding his face as his seed spurted out on to Olympia's bare flesh.

'Oh, Madame, Madame.' He was almost weeping with shame, convinced that he had failed in his task. Meanwhile, Olympia was thinking exactly the same thing about herself. What if she could not bring him to exquisite pleasure inside her? What if he returned to the Légionnaires with tales of failure and disillusionment? She thought of using the oil on him, but it was so powerful that she feared it would only make matters worse. No, she must find some other, subtler way to pleasure her little tiger cub. She must rely solely upon the sensual armoury of her natural skills.

'Hush, hush,' she soothed, smoothing cool hands over his fretful body; and he sank back on to the bed, giving himself up to the strength of Olympia's passionate determination.

Kneeling on the bed between his thighs, she began teasing him with the point of her skilful tongue, nipping his taut young flesh between her sharp little teeth, so adeptly that he flinched and sighed, not quite sure if he was feeling pleasure or pain.

The flesh between his thighs began to stir once more, but did not yet become erect. On a sudden impulse, Olympia stopped tormenting the boy, and rolled on to her back. After a few moments, he too rolled over, raised himself on to his elbows and stared down at Olympia, completely baffled.

'*Madame Olympia, qu'est-ce qui see passe?* Why have you stopped? It was so nice.'

She laughed.

'I'm sure it was, *chéri*. But I think it is now time for you to play with *my* body for a little while.'

'But Madame, *je ne sais comment*, I cannot!'

'Have you never pleasured a woman before, *petit tigre*?'

He reddened with embarrassment and shame.

'*Jamais, Madame Olympia.* Never have I even seen a naked woman before.'

'Then now is the time for you to learn, *non*?'

Gently, she took hold of the boy's hand; it was

trembling as she guided it with slow deliberation to the hardening crests of her nipples.

'These are my little rosebuds of love, *tigre*. They tell my lovers when I am ready for them. Can you feel how they harden at your touch?'

The boy nodded, spellbound, as Olympia's nipples grew firm and erect, even at his clumsy touch. There was a rough charm in the boy's innocent awkwardness, mused Olympia, warming to the game. She felt relaxed now, and randy. It felt as though the aphrodisiac oil she had been handling had soaked right into her very bones, and an irresistible warmth was radiating through her entire body. She gave a little murmur of pleasure as the boy's fingers brushed her nipples, then grew bolder and began gently pinching the flesh.

'That's it, *chéri*. Gently but firmly. Ouch! Not quite so hard. Now let me show you another trick to please your lady friend.'

She seized his hand again, and this time guided it down her belly to the luxuriant forest of her pubis, still fragrant with the warm oils, showing him how to stroke and tease the hair, winding the red-gold curls around his fingers.

'Yes, that's it – *exactement comme ça*. If you do that for your girlfriend, *p'tit tigre*, you will make her growl like a real tigress. Now, give me your finger, and we'll go exploring. There! See how it opens up, like a flower?'

'So wet!' exclaimed the boy, amazed at the abundance of love-juice oozing from Olympia's most secret places. 'Like . . . like . . .'

'Like a tropical rainforest,' purred Olympia. 'Where the still, slow river runs between banks of bright foliage, dripping with moisture, and the whole forest is teeming with life. *C'est ça, n'est-ce pas?* Feel the life in me, little tiger. Feel how the waters rise at your touch.'

Gently, she guided his fingertip so that it was on the very mount of her desire.

'Stroke the flower-bud,' she gasped, her own desire getting the better of her now. 'And see how ripe and full of sweet sap it is.'

He obeyed, almost mechanically, as though he were in a trance of lustful disbelief. Disbelief that this could be reality; that he could really be lying on this bed, in this luxurious hotel room, pleasuring a beautiful golden-haired woman at her command.

As she felt the storm of passion gathering within her, Olympia forced herself to take the young boy's finger from her clitoris.

'You have seen and felt my sap,' she whispered. 'Now you shall taste it.'

And she bent his head down until it was between her thighs.

'Lap, my tiger. Lap at the sweet, life-giving waters.'

Instinctively, he put out his tongue and began licking at her, to such good effect that, within a few seconds, Olympia felt herself approaching the summit of her pleasure. Holding his face pressed close against her womanhood, she came, love-juice flooding out of her and in between his astonished lips.

'Madame, Madame!' babbled the boy as she released him from his delightful prison. 'Never have I . . . never . . .!'

His face was sticky and glistening with her juices, and she kissed him passionately, full on the

195

lips, revelling in her own unmistakable taste and scent.

She glanced down, and saw that her stratagem had worked to excellent effect, just as she had planned. The boy was stiff and ready for her, his eager young manhood taut as a longbow, about to release its deadly arrow.

'Take me,' she whispered in the boy's ear as she pulled him down on top of her. 'Take me, my little tiger. I want to feel your claws.'

He was an unprepossessing sight, and Olympia groaned inwardly. A tall, thin man in a long black coat, there were dark circles round his sunken eyes, and his unnaturally pale skin had a touch of the troglodyte about it. Or the vampire.'

Banishing such foolish thoughts, she ushered the ghoulish figure into her room, praying that he would not exact too terrible a price from her tired flesh. The last stranger had made her enact disturbing fantasies which still spun round in her brain.

The man sat down in one of the armchairs, and produced a bottle of red wine, which he uncorked and placed carefully on the table.

'A simple vin rouge,' he said, without a trace of a smile. 'I so love the rich redness, the slightly metallic taste . . . it reminds me of blood, and blood reminds me of both life and death. In my line of work, I need to feel at ease with dead flesh.'

'W-what *is* your line of work?'

'Why, I am an undertaker of course, dear lady.' For the first time, he smiled. It was a horrible, thin-lipped smile that exposed his irregular teeth and reminded Olympia of a death's-head rictus. 'And I

196

do so love my work. It gives me such pleasure. I wonder if you will give me as much.'

Olympia shivered, and sank into the chair opposite.

'Your pleasure is my only aim,' she replied, aware that her voice must sound hollow and mechanical. 'Whatever it is that you desire, you have only to ask.'

When she saw him open his small leather case and take out a noose of thick rope, she almost fainted with fright. Did he intend her harm? Did he intend to use it on her? And then he pulled open the noose, and placed it neatly around his neck, tightening it slightly so that the knot was hanging under the left side of his chin.

'The position of the knot is vitally important,' he continued, as casually as if he were a mechanic explaining the workings of a carburettor. 'If it is not placed directly under the chin, the neck may not be broken instantly, and the victim will suffer a long and agonising death by strangulation . . . and of course, there is the length of the drop to take into consideration.' Olympia shrank away from his gaze, hoping he wasn't making any calculations on her behalf.

The man's eyes glittered with suppressed excitement as he continued: 'You know, it has been claimed by some that, at the moment of death by hanging or decapitation, a man experiences the most tremendous orgasm of his entire life. Do you not think death would be a price worth paying, to enjoy the secrets of such unparalleled pleasure?'

He trailed the end of the rope over his crotch, and Olympia saw that the mere thought had made him rampant with lust.

Suddenly, with a great rush of relief, Olympia realised what he was trying to tell her. He had no intention of using the noose on her. He wanted her to understand his obsession with death so that she could use it to gratify him!

'Take off your clothes,' commanded Olympia, doing her best to sound authoritative.

Plainly delighted, the undertaker slipped off his coat and the starched, wing-collared shirt with the black silk cravat. She helped him off with his polished boots and black breeches; then he stepped out of his underpants and stood naked before her. He was an almost spectral figure, unnaturally thin and very, very pale, as though he shunned the daylight. But his manhood was large, hard and vigorous, almost as though all the energy within his frail body had gone into nurturing and sustaining it.

'Kneel.'

He obeyed, and she tightened the noose about his scrawny neck until it exerted a firmer pressure on his windpipe. Instantly he grew visibly more erect, and she heard his breathing quicken. Then she cast around for other props to use in her little charade. The rectangular stool from the dressing table, she pushed it in front of him with her foot.

'Bend over it. Hold on to the sides tightly.'

The leather belt from the undertaker's trousers made an acceptable whip, and Olympia set about flaying him as energetically as she had Monsignor Testi, the day before in the basement of the antique shop. The undertaker seemed to enjoy the experience, for as his back and buttocks coloured to a marbled red and white, he began moaning quietly to himself and clutching convulsively at the stool which supported him.

Olympia could see that his pleasure was near, and advanced the scene towards its final, dramatic act.

'You are a wicked man, Monsieur.'

'Oh yes, yes, very wicked.'

'You deserve to be punished.'

'Punishment. Punish me, punish me.'

'Do you think you deserve . . . to die?'

The words had an electric effect on the under-taker, and he rolled his eyes Heavenwards in an expression of extreme distress.

'Oh yes, yes. Death is the only penalty for my sins. I must die. I must die now!'

'Very well. Then die you shall!'

Seizing the wine bottle and lifting it shoulder-high, Olympia let the blood-red fluid cascade down on to the miserable undertaker's head. As he saw the wine running down over the stool, he let out a thin scream; and at that moment, she brought down the belt upon the back of his neck with a stinging blow, emulating the blade of the guillotine or the executioner's axe.

'Die, wretch! Die!'

With a juddering sigh, he fell forwards on to the stool, arms outstretched as if in death. For a moment, Olympia wondered if perhaps she had indeed killed him, dealing him such a shock that his heart had given out. But then he began to moan and gasp, and, turning him over with her foot, she saw that his joy had spurted out all over the hotel carpet, mingling pearly semen with cheap red wine. She would have a lot more explaining to do to Monsieur Constant Faillou.

* * *

Olympia glanced at the clock on the bedside table. Eight-thirty. The last stranger had left fifteen minutes ago, and the messenger would be here at nine. She gave a sigh of relief. The undertaker must have been the last of her visitors.

She was just enjoying a few moments of self-congratulation when there was a knock on the door.

Reluctantly, she hauled herself to her feet and went to the door. Outside stood a man in a grey uniform, with a small padded envelope in his gloved hand.

'Mademoiselle Deschamps?'

'*Entrez, entrez.* Do hurry, please – there isn't much time left!'

She grabbed him by the shoulder and dragged him bodily into the room.

'What . . .?'

'There's no time to argue! Just get your clothes off. Go on! *Déshabillez-vous – et vite!*'

With a shrug of his shoulders, the man began undressing. He had a reasonably good body, mused Olympia, and she wouldn't have minded spending some time exploring it, but they were here for his pleasure, not hers.

As he lay down on the bed and she straddled him with her still-eager thighs, Olympia hoped against hope that she would succeed in pleasuring this final visitor before the messenger arrived. It was such a shame to hurry the delights of the flesh. And her partner was such a promising subject. She only hoped he was enjoying himself as much as she was.

With only seconds to spare, the stranger groaned in pleasure and Olympia sank on to him exhausted. She did not even hear the knock at the door.

'*Mon Dieu*, Olympia – you certainly have an awesome appetite!'

Olympia raised her head to survey the messenger, framed in the doorway and grinning all over his face.

'What do you mean? And what's so amusing? I completed the task, didn't I?'

The messenger came into the room and closed the door behind him. Prone on the bed beneath her, the stranger gave a faint groan but did not move.

'Most assuredly you did, *ma chère*. I was merely alluding to your present conquest. I should have thought that, after a night of arduous pleasure, you would have wanted to rest. Such enthusiasm is indeed laudable in an aspiring Légionnaire.'

'You mean . . . are you telling me that this is not one of the strangers the Légion sent to me?' She stared down at the visitor, who now had a blissful smile on his face.

'I'm afraid not. You have just screwed my motor-cycle courier, Olympia. This gentleman was merely the postman. I believe he has a small packet for you. Ah yes.' He picked the padded envelope up off the floor, and tore it open. 'For you, Mademoiselle.'

She took the contents and looked at them in puzzlement.

'A blank video cassette? What's this for?'

'It is for the next trial, Olympia. And one which I feel sure you will enjoy. Why don't you read the card?'

Olympia slid the card out of its envelope and read it.

Congratulations, Olympia. Thus far you have done yourself credit. But tomorrow night you face your greatest challenge yet. Using the enclosed video-tape, you must obtain film of yourself performing in a live sex-show in a Paris night club. Good fortune in your quest.

Chapter Ten

'A nd so you see, Caroline, I need some help.'
    Olympia sat back in her chair and sipped a citron pressé, watching the world go by on the sunlit boulevard.

'It all sounds very mysterious, Olympia. Why won't you tell me what this is all about?'

'I wish I could, Caroline; but believe me, it's safer if you don't know.'

Caroline took a swig from her umpteenth pastis and pulled on a Gauloise.

'Now, let's get this straight. You want me to help you get a part in a live sex show in some crummy nightclub in the red-light district. And then you want me to help you video your starring performance – have I got that right?'

'More or less, yes.'

'Hmm. It's audacious, even for you, Olympia. I take it you've abandoned all this nonsense about celibacy – I told you that massage would make you think again, didn't I? Sometimes, I just can't make you out. Look, I'll have a word with my friend Léon. I should think he's quite well up on the seedy backstreet clubs, being a total sleazeball himself, but I can't promise that he'll know anybody really useful. And even if we do get you fixed up with a début at the Club Zizi, what about the video?'

'How do you mean?'

'The filming, darling. Have you got a camcorder?'

'Of course not. I thought we could hire one.'

'Fine. And when we've hired it, who's going to use it? Because if you think I'm going to be seen dead in some red-light dive with a camcorder on my shoulder, creasing my best black Versace, you're very much mistaken.' She thought for a moment. 'Didn't you say that boy of yours . . . Joachim is it? Didn't you say he was a bit of a dab hand with a camera?'

'It's worth a try, I suppose,' conceded Olympia. 'But I don't know how I'm going to explain it to him.'

Caroline laughed, and drained her glass.

'Good God, Olympia – tell him it's art! And besides; did you ever meet a man who'd turn down a visit to a live sex-show?'

That afternoon, Caroline returned to the hotel with a list of clubs which had live sex-shows scheduled for the following evening. The first on the list was a back-street club in Pigalle.

'Do I look OK?' asked Olympia nervously, adjusting her strapless black bustier so that it showed off her figure to best advantage.

'Like a complete tart, darling,' replied Caroline, acidly.

'Oh good,' smiled Olympia. 'That's exactly how I wanted to look.'

'Léon says it's an absolute dive, you know; so I just hope you know what you're doing, that's all,' grumbled Caroline as Olympia strode towards the intimidating entrance to the Perroquet Rose.

'If you're scared, you can leave now. It's OK, I'll manage on my own.' Olympia gave Caroline one of her defiant stares and tried to look brave. But she was relieved when Caroline shrugged and replied:

'It's OK, I'm here now. And somebody's got to make sure you don't get yourself into more trouble than you're already in.'

Loud knocking on the door produced no response for ages, and they were about to leave and try another club on Léon's list when at last they heard footsteps in the distance.

The door opened a few inches, to reveal a massively-built man who glared at them suspiciously.

'*Que voulez-vous?*'

'Oh, excuse me,' purred Olympia, trying to simper. 'We're here for the auditions.'

'Auditions? We're not holding any auditions.'

'Oh dearie me,' broke in Caroline. 'That's very strange. My friend Monsieur Broussin was quite sure that you'd be wanting some really classy girls for tomorrow night's show. And my friend here is *very* experienced in this line of work.'

'I see.' There was a short silence. 'Well, I suppose you'd better come in. But I can't say if Herr

205

Gutenberg will see you. Very important man, is our Herr Gutenberg.'

With much sliding of bolts and rattling of chains, the two women were ushered into the cavernous depths of the Perroquet Rose by their host, a burly ex-boxer called Hervé.

The club was the height of kitsch, done out like a nineteenth-century tart's boudoir, Caroline observed as they walked past the padded pink satin couches and little gilded tables. The dance-floor was dominated by a huge plaster parrot, which hung from the ceiling on golden chains, and all round it were little swings, like gilded trapezes.

The walls were covered in bright pink watered silk, hung with *fin-de-siècle* photographs of wide-eyed nymphettes, coyly displaying their naked-ness to a largely indifferent world.

'Olivier was right,' hissed Olympia as they walked through this wonderland of bad taste. 'It *is* a dive. It's perfect.'

At the far end of the club was the stage: a raised platform, from the centre of which emerged a long catwalk, which extended some ten or fifteen yards into the audience, at eye level. Caroline nudged Olympia, and observed laconically: 'Strut your stuff up there, darling, and they'll be able to see right up your knickers.'

Olympia giggled.

'Who says I'm wearing any?'

They reached a candy-pink door spangled with silver stars, and their burly companion wiped his hands on a stained white apron before knocking on it, rather timorously for a man of his obvious presence.

A muffled grunt from beyond the door indicated

that the club owner was not pleased at being disturbed.

'What is it now, Hervé? I told you I'm busy.'

'Herr Gutenberg,' wheedled the boxer. 'I have two very attractive young ladies here with me. They say they want to audition for tomorrow night's sex-show.'

'Tell them I don't need any more girls,' retorted Herr Gutenberg.

'But sir, they say they're very experienced.'

There was a long pause, then the door swung inwards. A fat, balding man appeared in the doorway, buckling up his trouser belt. As Olympia peered over his shoulder into the dingy office beyond, she caught sight of an extremely brassy blonde in fishnet stockings, pulling down her skirt.

Olympia gave him her most seductive smile.

'We've come a long way,' she pleaded. 'Everybody says the Perroquet Rose is *the* sex show in town.'

The club owner looked her up and down, with a faint awakening of interest. The brassy blonde was now standing behind him, chewing gum and giving the two interlopers a hostile glare. Herr Gutenberg scratched his bald head thoughtfully.

'English?'

'Through and through,' replied Caroline, helpfully pushing Olympia in front of her. 'Actually, it's my friend here who wants to audition – she's had much more experience of this sort of thing than I have.'

Fibber, thought Olympia, remembering the time Caroline had taken a job as a stripagram girl to pay off her enormous account at Emporio Armani. Dressed up as a policewoman, with black seamed

207

stockings and a short, short skirt, Caroline had certainly given her victims a lot more than just a strict caution.

'Oh, go on,' continued Caroline, flashing Herr Gutenberg a laser-beam smile that would vapourise granite. 'Do audition her for your show. In the Swedish sex clubs, they call her English Rose.'

'English girls are frigid,' butted in the brassy blonde, with venom. Olympia noticed that her scarlet lipstick had smudged all over her teeth. 'Everyone knows that, Otto. You don't want to employ some toffee-nosed English bitch who looks like she's got a bad smell under her nose.'

'Shut up, Ingrid,' snarled Gutenberg, weighing up the possibilities of these two English beauties. 'So they're a pair of snooty bitches – but they're classy with it. Maybe the punters would enjoy a bit of class for a change. And besides, they're not frigid, you can see they're a pair of right little goers – aren't you, ladies?' He dealt Caroline a hearty slap on the backside.

'Like I said, it's just my friend here,' broke in Caroline, uneasily.

Herr Gutenberg shook his head sadly.

'Well, now, that's a real pity 'cos I'm only looking for a double act, see. It's both of you together, or I'm not interested. Got it, girls?'

Caroline and Olympia exchanged glances.

'No way,' said Caroline.

'Oh please, Caroline. For me.'

'Uh-oh.'

'You might enjoy it.'

'In the Club Apollo on the Boulevard Haussman, maybe. But in a seedy little dive like this? Not in a million years.'

'I might have to tell Francesca about that time you spent the night with her husband on their water-bed.'

Caroline sighed. 'Oh all right, then. But you owe me one, Olympia. Don't you ever forget that!'

Olympia smiled sweetly at Herr Gutenberg, kissed her fingertip and placed it on his pendulous lower lip. In the background, Ingrid quietly seethed with jealousy.

'What would you like us to do for our audition, Herr Gutenberg? We're *very* versatile.'

Otto turned to his blonde mistress.

'Go and get Marco and Alessandro. Hurry now, I haven't got all day.'

Reluctantly Ingrid flounced off through a pink silk-padded door and reappeared a few minutes later with two olive-skinned hunks clad only in the briefest of skin-tight cycling shorts. They had been exercising, and their tanned skin was sprinkled with little beads of sweat.

'Two little English Roses for you, boys. Go ahead. You can do anything you like with them,' instructed Gutenberg, pulling up a chair and sitting down with Ingrid on his lap and his podgy hand up her red polka-dot skirt. 'It's their audition for tomorrow night's show. I want to see something really classy.'

Olympia needed little bidding, for the two lads were enough to inspire any red-blooded woman: tall and tanned, with a natural olive glow to their smooth, perfectly-toned skin. She ran an eager hand down Alessandro's magnificent torso, moulding the flesh, sensing the strength beneath the smoothness; and she pressed her lips against it, running her tongue over his salty skin, drinking in his sweat. Its bitter taste awoke deep, dark thirsts within her, and she sank to her knees before him, kissing him through the thin, sheer fabric of his cycling shorts.

He stood there like a statue as she tongued him through the flimsy fabric; but he was far from indifferent to her ministrations, for he was growing, flowering at her touch. She could feel the warmth of his excitement radiating into her as she took the swelling outline of his hardness between her lips and gently teased it with the sharpness of her teeth.

Behind her, she could hear Caroline moaning softly as Marco awoke her body to some secret, sensual touch, but Olympia was far too wrapped up in her own – and Alessandro's – pleasure to pay much attention to her friend.

Alessandro's muscular thighs were hard as stone beneath her fingers; and now his manhood was turning to stone, too, under the force of his desire. But still he stood before her, seemingly unmoved, like a beautiful sculpture, and only the swelling hardness between Olympia's lips betrayed the depth of his emotion.

Determined to conquer this passive resistance, Olympia took hold of the waistband of Alessandro's shorts and wrenched them down. His stiff penis sprang out eagerly, but she did not immediately take it into her mouth. Instead, to his surprise, she stood up and began to undress in front of him, achingly slowly. At last, clad only in strapless bustier, stockings and suspenders, she knelt before him once again, taking hold of his erect hardness as gently and reverentially as if it were a wounded bird, and planting sweet kisses on the tip. Then she pressed her breasts tightly against his groin, so that the hardened shaft slipped easily into the soft furrow between them. At last he gave a little sigh, the first audible sign of his pleasure.

Meanwhile, Marco was having great fun with his English ingénue.

'The English love pain,' he told Caroline with a smile as she sat on his lap, covering his neck with kisses. 'The whole world knows that. Who am I to deprive you of your pleasure?'

With that, he flipped Caroline neatly over on to her front and pulled up her skirt, exposing a pair of elegantly rounded buttocks inadequately covered by her little black G-string.

'All ready for me, I see, Signorina!'

He raised his hand and brought it down with such force that Caroline almost leapt into the air with the shock – and the indignity.

'Get off me, you horrible man!' she exclaimed, wriggling under the tormenting hand. 'I have not been spanked since I was seven years old, and I don't intend to start now!'

Despite her best efforts to escape, Marco's superior strength triumphed and she simply could not struggle free. Red-faced and indignant, she submitted to the indignity with extremely bad grace.

Olympia was having a much better time of it, and was thoroughly enjoying the spectacle of Alessandro's crumbling resolve as she rubbed her firm breasts against his hardened shaft. As she felt him about to come, she moved away from him, and watched his seed spurting out in hot, white jets on to the floor of the club.

211

Herr Gutenberg, watching from his ringside seat, applauded the spectacle with genuine enthusiasm.

'Bravo, ladies!' he declared. 'No one's seduced our Alessandro quite so artistically for a long time. And the spanking tableau – so picturesque! So amusing, yet so titillating!'

Bottle-blonde Ingrid pouted her disapproval, and dodged the clumsy kiss he wanted to plant on her cheek.

'Well, I thought they were useless, Otto – really ordinary.'

'That's a pity, Ingrid, because I'm going to hire them both for tomorrow's night's show. So you'd better get used to the idea.'

Ingrid gave a sly, triumphant smile.

'Well, Otto, here's something *you'd* better get used to. If you hire those two English bitches, I'm going to bring all the other girls out on strike! And the boys, too. What will you do then, eh? You can't run a sex show without any performers.'

Olympia sighed. Her plans were not working out at all as she'd expected. It's one thing to be rejected because you aren't good enough, but being fired because the boss's floosie thinks you're too sexy is a bit much for a girl to bear. And she was running out of time.

She poured Caroline yet another Pernod, and sat back to watch her gulp it down, fascinated by her friend's seemingly inexhaustible capacity to drink without ever getting drunk.

'What am I going to do now?' she groaned.

'Try another club, darling. There's always tomorrow night.'

212

'No there isn't, Caroline. It has to be tonight, or not at all. You don't understand.'

'That's hardly surprising, dear, since you keep refusing to explain what's going on.'

'I'm sorry. But I can't tell you. It might put you in danger.'

Caroline thought for a while, then an idea came to her.

'Tell you what, Olympia. Why don't we get tickets for Herr Gutenberg's sex show tonight?'

'What's the use? We'd be sitting in the audience, not performing on stage.'

Caroline threw her head back and laughed.

'Haven't you ever heard of audience participation?'

Joachim stretched out in bed and took a sip from his glass of wine.

'You're a very unusual woman, Olympia Deschamps. And a very mysterious one.'

Olympia cuddled up close and put her arm round her young lover, drinking in his warmth. Already she was hungry for love again.

'Please trust me, Joachim. I'd tell you if I could, really I would. But it's better that you don't know. Won't you help me?' She stroked his flank, instinctively knowing his sensual triggers even better than he knew them himself. 'All you have to do is sit in the audience and point a camcorder at me.'

'Well, I won't say I'm not puzzled, *chérie*.' He rolled round to face Olympia and took her in his arms, closing her eyes with little playful kisses. 'But then again, I won't say I'm not excited, either. You think of such pretty games to play.'

'Excited?' Olympia rubbed herself up against

him, her nipples hardening with the rough contact of his wiry hair.

'*Mais certainement!* I enjoyed watching you with the priest, *p'tit chou*; and making love with you in the toilettes at the Grand Louvre; and I've no doubt at all that I'll enjoy watching you taking your clothes off in a live sex-show. You know, there's something very sexy about seeing your lover in the arms of another man. You're a crazy woman, Olympia Deschamps – but I just can't get you out of my head.'

'I'll always come back to you,' breathed Olympia, crushing her mouth against his. 'Always, my darling.'

'I know you will, *chérie*. How could I doubt it?' Joachim's hands were strong yet skilful on her body; an artist's hands, with the sure touch of the sculptor who coaxes beauty and joy from the cold, unliving stone.

'Make love to me again, Joachim,' sighed Olympia. At this moment, she longed to surrender to another's will; to allow another to pleasure her as she lay in his strong arms. She could not always be invincible, magnificent; sometimes she just wanted to lie back and be loved, like the timorous, virginal heroine in a romantic novelette.

And so, this afternoon she would relax in Joachim's gentle arms. But tonight, she would once again become Olympia the huntress.

The Perroquet Rose was an altogether livelier place by night. Outside, a huge and very garish billboard announced: LIVE SEX ACTION – TONITE! MISS INGRID AND HER SEXY SISTERS

Caroline and Olympia showed their tickets and

membership cards at the door and went inside. Whatever its pretensions might be, this was no high-class night-club for the glitterati, and – apart from the hostesses – women were few and far between. Under the weird glow from hundreds of candy-pink lightbulbs, the club looked ever seedier than it had seemed that afternoon.

Naked girls with pink feather headdresses like tufts of candyfloss, perched daintily on the gilded trapezes, whilst waitresses in high heels and sickly-pink ostrich feathers plied the clientele with over-priced pink champagne. In one corner of the club, a group of drunken workmen on a stag night were touching up one of the hostesses, who was screeching with laughter as the groom-to-be poured champagne down the front of her tight pink dress.

Caroline and Olympia took their seats near the end of the catwalk, and watched the show for a while, until the club filled up and the acts really got going. Glancing across to the other side of the club, Olympia caught Joachim's eye, and he nodded. Everything was ready.

As Olympia had expected, the floor-show was as dire as the decor. Miss Ingrid was dressed up in satin shorts, fishnet tights and a blonde curly wig, like a third-class Dietrich. Sitting astride a chair in the middle of the stage, she pretended to pleasure a series of hunky male dancers with her capacious mouth. Drunks in the audience cheered each new success half-heartedly, but you could tell their hearts weren't in it. Ingrid's performance was hardly realistic or inspiring. Meanwhile, in the background, Ingrid's 'sexy sisters' did a rather innocent little topless dance routine with Marco and Alessandro. This was not Olympia's idea of 'live sex action'. Surely she could do better, and send the punters home happy.

Ingrid got up from her chair and strutted along to the end of the catwalk, tormenting the drunken men who reached up and tried to grab her, then pausing for a moment to unhook her black satin bra and fling it into the audience. She didn't seem to have noticed her two deadly rivals at the end of the catwalk, waiting to strike. As she turned her back on them for a brief moment, Olympia hissed to Caroline:

'Now, I think. Yes – go for it!'

Caroline hooked the handle of her umbrella around Ingrid's ankle with consummate ease. The four-inch red stilettos gave her no chance against Caroline's determined assault, and Ingrid hardly had time to give a squeal of alarm before she stumbled, overbalanced and fell headlong into the sea of baying punters, arms flailing in a vain attempt to save herself from disaster.

Standing in the wings, Herr Gutenberg looked on in consternation as his brassy starlet Ingrid disappeared into a mass of lust-crazed drunks who evidently thought free sex with Ingrid was part of the show. Gutenberg, for one, had no intention of trying to persuade them to give up their prize, and it was obvious that Ingrid was going to be fully occupied for the rest of the evening. The show was in chaos. Ingrid's 'sisters' were wandering about in a daze, and the pretty boys had no one to do their act with. This was a disaster!

'Now's your chance,' said Caroline. 'Get up there and do your stuff!'

Without further ado, Olympia hauled herself up

on to the catwalk. As she got to her feet, she glanced over in Joachim's direction and saw the lens of the camcorder, glinting among the audience. Right, she thought to herself: lights, camera – action!

Herr Gutenberg's eyes almost popped out of their sockets as the girl with the red-gold hair and the perfect breasts got up on to the catwalk. She was wearing the same black leather bustier and skirt that she'd worn for the audition, and he recognised her instantly.

'*Himmel* – it's English Rose!'

'Shall I have her thrown out, Sir?' demanded Hervé, rolling up his sleeves.

'Good God no. Leave her be, Hervé. She may just save this evening from being a complete fiasco.'

Seated in the audience, agents from the Légion d'Amour watched with keen interest as Olympia began a long, slow, tantalising strip which had the audience breathless with excitement.

'She's a spirited girl,' remarked the magistrate, remembering how good it had felt to have her cool, firm hands on his ageing flesh. 'Full of confidence and panache. The perfect exhibitionist.'

'Hmm, yes, but I have yet to be convinced that the Deschamps girl is suitable Légion material,' replied the physician. 'She's a handsome young woman, I grant you, but as yet I have seen insufficient evidence of her powers to seduce and excite.'

Olympia, the blushing English rose, was now naked save for her knee-length, spike-heeled boots, and the punters' eyes were gleaming with lust for the glorious, unattainable, golden flesh that whirled and danced before them as the band played on. There was a dainty little silver-handled whip in her skilful grasp, and each time beseeching hands reached out to touch her she danced nimbly away, rewarding their devotion with the burning kiss of the lash's tip.

She taunted the pretty dancing-boys with her beauty and skill, stroking and kissing their yearning flesh until they almost wept with frustrated desire; and the girls looked on from afar, sensing that in Olympia Deschamps they had met their nemesis.

At last, Olympia scanned the audience for a partner. The thrill of power was in her belly as she surveyed the rows of men, all willing her to choose them. And she remembered that night at the Théâtre de la Timbale, when Michel Laloupe had enjoyed the self-same sense of power over his willing victims. A ripple of excitement ran round the club as her eyes lighted on a tall man with distinguished grey hair. He would do. He would do very well indeed.

The physician started and exchanged a meaningful glance with his companion as he realised that Olympia's eyes were on him. She was beckoning to him to join her up there, on the catwalk. For an instant, her green eyes seemed to scour the very depths of his soul, and then she bent down to take his hand and pulled him upon to the catwalk beside her. A moment ago, he had been a mere spectator; now he was part of the performance. Soon, he would be her naked, willing victim, as she had once been Laloupe's.

'You're mine, now,' she explained as she forced him to his knees between her outspread thighs.

'Mine to do with exactly as I wish. And first of all, I wish you to pleasure me with your tongue.'

She shivered with pleasure as she felt the strong hands on her thighs; the warmth of his kisses on her love-lips.

As for the physician, if he had had any doubts at all, they melted clean away as he pressed his face close to Olympia's red-gold curls and tasted the honeydew of her sweet, succulent womanhood.

Olympia tried to concentrate on the magazine article, but it was impossible to tear her thoughts away from the previous night at the Perroquet Rose.

What a triumph it had been. How pleased she had been to see the messenger outside the stage door of the club, waiting to take away the video-tape, the indisputable proof of Olympia's success. And how excited young Joachim had been by her daring exploits. So excited, that they had made passionate love through the sultry Paris night. This morning he was leaving for London, to set up the exhibition, and there was an ache of loss in the pit of her stomach. She was going to miss him dreadfully.

Still, there were other matters requiring her urgent attention. In a few moments, she was going to discover the substance of the final task. The very last one! She was so close, now, to achieving her dream. She could not, simply must not, fail. To do so would be to betray the memory of her beloved, brilliant father. Her father, who had died so many years ago, leaving Olympia to carry on his life's quest. She wished he could see her now: he would be so proud of his only daughter.

The clock ticked past nine o'clock, and she began to wonder if the messenger would ever come. Time seemed to pass so slowly, like thick, yellow honey dripping languidly from a cold teaspoon. She sat back in the armchair, closing her eyes and trying to stop her heart pounding.

The knock almost made her leap out of the chair in fright. Heart in her mouth, she stood up, straightened her clothes and went to welcome the messenger. The door lock was fiddly this morning, and her trembling fingers fumbled with the chain. At last the door opened.

'Come with me,' commanded the stranger, his face obscured by a leather mask that covered the entire head, leaving only ugly holes for his eyes, nose and mouth. The same black leather encased his body, and for a fleeting moment Olympia almost believed he was some strange creature from another, more sinister world.

'But why? What . . .?'

'No questions,' snapped the stranger, attaching handcuffs to her wrists. 'Today, you are mine. Mine to deal with in any way I please.'

Chapter Eleven

*A*t first, Olympia scarcely understood what was happening to her. But as the long, black limousine purred through the Paris streets, realisation slowly dawned. This really was her final trial: the ultimate ordeal which would determine whether or not she would be admitted to the Légion d'Amour.

She lay silent and unmoving on the back seat, the blindfold depriving her of any sense of where she was being taken. Fear gnawed at her heart; an ordinary woman's fear of weakness, of loss of control.

The man's words went round and round in her head.

'You are mine now. Mine to do with as I wish. Today, you shall be the slave of my every desire. The only limits are the limits of your own fear . . .'

What did it all mean? And would she be able to meet the challenges which would be placed in her path today? As the limo glided round a corner and began bumping over cobble stones, Olympia's mind drifted back to the time when, as a teenager, she and her friends had 'kidnapped' one of the teachers at their secretarial college, for a rag-week fundraising stunt.

Of course, it had been meant to be a bit of fun, but somehow it had got out of hand. The teacher was young and devastatingly handsome, and in a funny sort of way his fear had been like an aphrodisiac to the young girls who became his captors.

He had been blindfolded, as she was now, and had been given no warning of what was going to happen to him. Only now could Olympia understand how horribly disorientated he must have felt – unable to see where he was, or who with. As time passed, maybe he had even begun to doubt his own identity.

They had meant to tell him that it was all a joke, really they had. They had meant to take the blindfold off his eyes the minute they got to the hideout, and ply him with champagne and chocolates until the 'ransom' was paid by a philanthropic friend of the college principal. But somehow it had been much more fun not to tell him; to let him believe that he really had been kidnapped.

Olympia felt the weight of her guilt now, as she lay on the back seat of the limo, helpless and apprehensive. She had wanted to tell the young teacher about the game, but she had been excited by his obvious fear. And she knew he had been excited by it, too because his body had responded joyfully to all their little torments.

You can torture someone with a feather. *Really* torture. He was in tears of agony as they let its fine tip dance over his bare flesh, sparing no part of his delicious young body. And when they had forced him to taste the agony of unnbearable excitement, they had soothed him with their tongues, and bitten gently into his firm, ripe flesh.

They had all had sex with him, even Olympia, who felt uneasy about the man's helplessness. For his pleasure was tainted by fear of what was going to happen to him. He wept as his unseen tormentors sat astride him, taking him brutally as men have so often taken women, without apology and without excuse. The only excuse was their pleasure. And all the time, even at the moment of climax, the girls had conducted themselves in perfect, flawless silence. He had never known the identity of the girls who kidnapped him.

In the end the 'ransom' had arrived and they delivered him, safe and sound but still blindfolded, back to the college. He never told anyone about what had really happened to him, about that one extraordinary day in his ordinary young life. He left soon after, and they never saw him again, but they did hear some time later that he had been sacked from his new job, for some sexual impropriety with a pupil. Olympia had often wondered if his actions had been affected by what they had done to him.

Now, a lifetime later, Olympia Deschamps was discovering what it was like to be on the other side of the blindfold. As the car wheels crunched on gravel, then jolted to a halt, she sensed that the moment she had been dreading had at last come. They had arrived at their destination.

Rough hands dragged her out of the car, setting her on her feet and making her walk across gravel, up stone steps, and through a heavy door that crashed behind her like the entrance to a cathedral.

Inside the building it was very cool, and the air smelt dank, as though no one used the building very much. What was it – a derelict house, a disused warehouse? A few more steps and they went through a door; then down, down, down a spiral staircase into somewhere very damp and cold. Olympia heard a key turn in the lock behind her. She felt dizzy, and shivered in her nakedness, knowing that she was infinitely vulnerable.

'Welcome, Olympia,' said the same cold, fascinating voice. 'We are so very glad to welcome you here, to the temple of your fears.'

'I don't understand. What do you mean, the temple of my fears?'

'Silence! You shall speak only when you are bidden. The penalty for transgression shall be three strokes of the lash.'

As though in illustration, Olympia felt a stinging sensation on her back as a whip snaked through the air.

All at once, the room seemed full of whispering voices. How many? She could not tell. Echoes muddled the sounds, so that she could pick out only isolated words.

'Bitch.'

'Sweet pain . . .'

'Slave of pleasure.'

'Hurt.'

'Fear.'

'Please!' exclaimed Olympia, trying unsuccessfuly to turn her face towards the voice. 'Please take off the blindfold.'

'Poor, sweet Olympia,' said the first voice again,

heavy with irony. 'She wants us to remove the blindfold.' Laughter burst out all around her, sinister and mocking, and she felt cold beads of sweat standing out on her skin. 'But my dear girl, that would entirely invalidate the experiment. And it would so spoil our fun.

'You see, Olympia, this is the temple of fear, where you shall confront your deepest and darkest terrors and, with our help, turn them into pleasures. Shall we begin? You feel hot; so very hot. Burning – the flames are going to consume you.'

At all once, Olympia felt an extreme heat surrounding her, and the sound of distant roaring and crackling, as of flames. How could they do this to her? Were the flames real, or was the whole thing an illusion, conjured up by hypnotic suggestion? Fear whispered to her that the flames were real, and she tried to shrink back, only to meet strong arms which gripped her so tightly that she cried out in alarm. She could feel the flames on her skin now, and her lungs were filling with suffocating smoke. Terrifying images raced through her disorientated mind.

'Fire, *chérie*. The inferno. Do you remember how afraid you were of fire when you were a child? Do you remember how you were shut in the barn one day, when the straw caught fire, and you thought that you would die?'

'No, please, no!' gasped Olympia as the heat intensified, forcing her to confront memories she had chased from her mind and hoped never to encounter again.

'Flames, Olympia. Fire and smoke. Can you feel the heat?'

Suddenly, as fear threatened to overwhelm her, the nature of the heat began to change. Something touched her again. A hand. Something cool and moist that grew warm as it touched the skin, then slowly began to heat up until it burned in the most delicious way. It was like being massaged with fire.

'Feel the flames licking at your flesh, Olympia. Feel how good it is to be at the heart of the inferno.'

Hands. Hands all over her, massaging, soothing, exciting, tormenting. She wanted to free herself from the torment, yet she knew she must endure.

At last, when she felt she could bear no more, the torment ended, as quickly as it had begun, leaving her aching and burning with a strange, unearthly desire. Once again the dull, damp air was playing across her bare flesh.

'Take it, Olympia. Take it and feel its power.'

The manacles were taken from her wrists, and something was placed in her hands. She recognised it straight away, and began to tremble.

'Afraid, Olympia. Afraid of the serpent?'

'No. No, never.'

She gritted her teeth and took the live snake, forcing herself to hold the sinuous creature as it writhed in hot, dry coils about her wrists.

'A cobra, Olympia. One drop of its venom would be deadly. You are afraid of snakes, aren't you? But wouldn't you like to feel its kiss on your firm, sweet flesh? The serpent loves you, Olympia. Feel how it yearns to plants its kiss on your throat.'

Olympia struggled to fight back her revulsion. How had these people succeeded in uncovering her deepest, darkest fears? Ever since childhood she had feared snakes. She had spent many an uncomfortable afternoon with one of her cousins – a thoroughly unpopular boy called Richard – who kept a vivarium in his bedroom. Tanks lined the walls, and there was a highly unpleasant stench of stale flesh about the whole place.

There were tanks that at first glance seemed empty, but closer inspection would always reveal some writhing or creeping horror, a lizard, watchful beneath a flat stone; huge, red-backed spiders with fat legs covered in russet-coloured hair; and of course the snakes, lying perfectly still on their bed of warm sand. A locust would crawl unwarily past a green gecko, blissfully unaware of its impending doom. Everything seemed watchful, expectant. Olympia had often felt as if it was she who was on display in a glass tank, not the spiders and snakes.

'Beautiful, aren't they?' Richard had held the red-legged tarantula in the palm of his hand, and caressed it as other, less enterprising, boys might stroke a pet mouse. 'Of course, you have to be careful when you're mating them – you can't keep the male and the female together for too long.'

'Why not?' Olympia had demanded naively.

'They eat each other.'

He had held the spider out to Olympia, but she shrank from the touch. 'There's no need to be a scaredy-cat,' he grinned. 'The bite isn't serious – well, not if you're careful.'

'What are these, then?' Olympia had asked as she turned to the contents of one of the other tanks, eager to change the subject.

'Black mambas,' explained Richard, with a macabre relish. 'Would you like to touch?'

'No!' exclaimed Olympia; but Richard was not about to countenance a refusal. Already he was reaching into the tank for the fattest, ripest specimen.

'Shouldn't you be wearing gloves or something?'

Richard laughed.

'Gloves are for amateurs. Besides, they wouldn't bite me. We have a very special relationship. I feed them, and they give me all their love, don't you, my darlings.'

He had scooped up one of the glossy black snakes, deftly handling it so that it lay in gently-pulsing coils about his forearm. He rubbed its head gently, and it seemed content.

'Go on – touch. You're not *scared*, are you? Girls are always scared. You're so *wet*.'

Goaded into recklessness by this accusation, Olympia had reached out and touched the mamba's head. To her surprise it was hot and dry, not cold and slimy as she had expected. Encouraged, she stroked it and it closed its eyes, as though in ecstasy.

'He likes you. You can hold him if you like.'

'Well . . . OK.'

Still highly dubious, but determined not to be outdone by her cousin, Olympia reached out and took the snake, letting it coil around her arms like a huge black bracelet. It was heavy and warm, and she had felt the life within it, pulsing like some hugely powerful engine.

After a while, the snake became too heavy to hold.

'I'm getting tired. I think you'd better have him back now.'

She had held out the snake to Richard; but as

228

the boy reached out to take it from her, its eyes snapped open in a glittering stare of purest hatred. Too slow to snatch his hands away, and too complacent to respond to the warning sign, Richard touched the mamba's head.

It's jaws opened and the glistening fangs darted out, stabbing through Richard's unwary flesh. Olympia could do nothing to help as he clutched his arm and cried out in pain and alarm.

The mamba, contented then, closed its eyes and slept in Olympia's arms.

The doctors did everything they could to save Cousin Richard, but it was too late. And ever since then, Olympia had had a pathological terror of snakes.

And now here she was, with a full-grown cobra coiling itself about her arms.

'Let it caress you, Olympia. It wants to explore you, to taste you.'

She knew that the command must be obeyed. But how? How could she bear to submit to the terror of the cobra's kiss? Then a picture of her father came into her mind. Her father, smiling and reassuring with his strong arm about her shoulders. 'You can do anything, Olympia. Anything – if you believe in yourself as I believe in you.'

Shivering, she relaxed her grip on the cobra and it coiled around her arm. She drew her arm closer to her body and the snake's head began a lazy exploration of her body; its warm, sleek head rubbing against the flesh of her belly, then moving upwards to the rounded swell of her breasts. At any moment, she expected its deadly tongue to dart out in a fatal kiss.

But the snake seemed lazy, well-fed. Perhaps it would not want to harm her, after all. Slowly, Olympia began to realise that the touch of the serpent's skin on hers was darkly sensual. The cobra seemed sensual, lascivious even; its interest in her was that of a lover, exploring his partner's body for the first time. The warm, dry scales slid over her skin with a delicious smoothness, and for the first time Olympia felt arousal stirring within her.

As though answering all her thoughts, she felt something brushing against her pubis. A hand? But it had a roughness to it. A leather-gloved hand, that was it, rubbing her love-lips with a rhythmic quality that was utterly impersonal – almost robotic. And yet so, so very pleasurable. She could never have dreamed of feeling sensual pleasure in such bizarre circumstances, such menacing surroundings; yet she could feel desire tightening her belly, moistening the secret garden between her thighs.

'Feel the serpent loving you, Olympia. Feel his kisses on your belly, your breasts, your throat.'

'Yes,' gasped Olympia, as the gloved hand disappeared between her thighs and hard, determined fingers began probing her most intimate softness. 'Oh, yes.'

'Feel the serpent's kisses as his head slips inside you.' At that moment, gloved fingers slipped inside Olympia's hot cave, and so perfect was the charade that for a few moments she truly believed it was the cobra's head between her thighs, making love to her. Love that was sublime because it was so perilous. Never had love and death been so inextricably linked.

230

The cobra's head rubbed over her breasts with a gentle, almost soothing rhythm. Dazed by pleasure, comforting thoughts began to filter into Olympia's consciousness. The Légion might wish to frighten her, as a test of endurance, but they would surely not wish to harm her. What would they do with her body if they accidentally killed her? People would ask uncomfortable questions. No – the snake was completely safe. Doubtless its fangs had been removed. She had heard that they sometimes did that with snakes in zoos and circuses. She could relax and let it caress her body with impunity.

In and out moved the gloved fingers, and still the cobra's head swayed rhythmically across her breasts, teasing her nipples into erect wakefulness. This was perfect pleasure; and Olympia cared nothing for the humiliation of it – of being watched by who knows how many lewd men in some dank Parisian basement. She would endure. And she would overcome.

Almost the point of climax, the fingers withdrew from her. She gave a groan of protest, but her distress was answered only with a curt laugh.

'No release for you, Olympia Deschamps. Not yet. You have yet to prove yourself worthy of it.

Strong arms took the cobra from her, and suddenly she felt bereft, alone, and very vulnerable. Without the reassuring warmth of its body, she felt cold and shivery. Her poor, abused clitoris was throbbing with the frustration of lust unfulfilled, and, realising that her wrists were no longer shackled, she slipped a hand slyly down her belly, towards the softly curling red-gold triangle of her pubic hair.

'No! I forbid it!'

The lash fell upon her bare back, and a sudden, brutal gesture tore her hand away from her pubis, wrenching her arm behind her back. Whimpering with the unexpected pain, she surrendered to superior strength.

'No pleasure until I allow it. Do you understand?'

'I . . . yes. I understand.'

'What are you, Olympia?'

'I . . . don't know.'

'You are my slave. You are nothing. From now on, you will call me Master, and I shall address you as Slave. Is that quite clear?'

'Yes, Master.'

Olympia stood silently before her master, unable to see him through the thick blindfold; her head bowed in a gesture of docile submission.

'Are you afraid of pain, Slave?'

'No, Master,' replied Olympia defiantly. 'I am afraid of nothing.'

'You lie!' Cruel fingers pinched her nipples very, very hard and she let out a little sigh of discomfort and surprise. 'There is no one on this earth who is unafraid of pain.' He paused. 'But some of us are able to welcome the pain, understand it and manipulate it, until at last it becomes pleasure.'

'Yes, Master.'

'Do not speak unless you are bidden.' A light slap on the cheek persuaded Olympia into rather sullen silence.

'I am going to remove your blindfold now, Slave. Do not attempt to run away, or your punishment will be severe. For the rest of today you shall serve my needs, and those of my friends. Do you understand?'

'I understand, Master.'

The gloved hands fumbled with the blindfold and released the knot. The scarf fell away from Olympia's eyes, and she blinked in the sudden light.

The room was not, as she had expected, some crumbling tenement in the red-light district, but what she realised at once was the crypt of a very ancient church. The low, vaulted ceiling exacerbated her intense feelings of claustrophobia, and the flickering light from candles and torches gave the place a thoroughly Gothic air. Dusty tombs and memorials lurked among the carved stone pillars, and gargoyles with grotesque faces grinned down at her from the ceiling.

There were four men in the room, all masked and clad in tight-fitting leather suits – dominant and threatening. They were sitting around a medieval tomb, its flat top laid out like a bizarre table, with glasses and plates as though for a banquet. The men's anonymity smacked to Olympia of cowardice, and in her contempt she forgot her master's command to remain silent.

'Why do you not show your faces? Is it because I know you? Or is it because you are afraid of discovery?'

The slender cane, flexible as a whiplash, struck her between the shoulder-blades and she let out a gasp of pain.

'I told you, Slave – hold your tongue!'

'Yes, Master.'

'I will not tell you a second time. You are

nothing. Your only identity shall be given to you by me.'

'I understand, Master.'

The one who had brought her to this place looked her up and down, then gave a dry laugh.

'No, my angry young miss; you do not know us – any of us. We have never met before, and it is unlikely that we shall ever meet again. Ours is destined to be a transient acquaintance – but a memorable one, I trust.' He ran his black-gloved hand over the red welts on Olympia's golden back. 'A little pain adds to the spice, don't you think?'

Before Olympia could answer, he turned away.

'Ours is an anonymous and impersonal love, my darling Slave. And you will in time come to comprehend the essential truth: that desire is a faceless, faithless creature, ever-changing, ever fickle. The identity of the partner is not important: all that matters is desire itself.'

He walked back to the table and indicated the three silent figures, sitting motionless before their macabre table.

'The hunger for life is an intense one, Slave. And desire is a deeper, subtler hunger within us all. An enduring appetite which should never leave us. The true sensualist hungers still, even when his appetite has been satisfied. Alas, all our appetites perish with us. We cannot take them beyond the grave. *Carpe diem*, sweet slave. Explore each hunger to its very limits, before death robs us of all desires, forever.'

Olympia stood in chastened silence, puzzled and yet strangely discomfited by this talk of hunger and death.

'Are you willing to explore that hunger, Slave?'

'I am willing, Master.'

'Excellent.' The Master sat down with his companions at the macabre table, and clapped his hands. 'We have need of refreshment, Slave. You will find wine on the floor over there. Select one of the bottles and pour the wine for us.'

Olympia walked through the crypt, in the direction that he had indicated. Over here it was darker, and cobwebs brushed off on her hair as she ducked beneath a low arch and found herself in what had once been a tiny chapel.

The chapel was little more than an alcove, with space for a small altar and three or four worshippers. But it seemed that no one had worshipped here for many years, for the place was covered in a thick layer of dust, and what had been the altar had decayed to a pile of rotting wood.

Olympia shivered, but entered the chapel. A single candle flickered beside the altar, and she saw something white lying on the floor beside it. Stooping down, she found a piece of card, inscribed with the message:

Desire is the only supreme truth. Worship the hunger within you.

Turning away in alarm, Olympia saw a neat row of wine bottles beside the wall, uncorked and ready for pouring. So her captors had even thought to let the wine breath before their little ceremony. How very civilised!

But which wine to choose? This was clearly a test of some kind. Olympia prided herself on her knowledge of fine wines, but how was she to read what was in her master's mind? Had he not emphasised the fickle nature of desire? Even if she anticipated his choice, he was quite likely to change his mind, simply out of spite.

She scanned the row of bottles. Twelve different wines, unlabelled but all excellent in their own way. Some extremely rare; some fresh and almost frivolous. A heavy, musky port wine; a light Beaujolais with the scent of summer meadows.

At last she settled on a Château Mouton Rothschild '86. Picking up the bottle, she left the chill of the abandoned chapel and made her way back towards the circle of light where her master and his friends still sat waiting for her, silent and motionless.

She approached with the bottle and took it straight to her master.

'You have chosen?'

'I have, Master.'

'I trust, for your sake, that it is a good choice. You may pour.'

The Master watched her like a hawk as she decanted a few drops of the precious fluid into his crystal glass. He held it up to the light, breathed in the bouquet and finally tasted it. Olympia held her breath and waited for retribution, certain that he would be dissatisfied with her choice.

To her amazement he put down his glass and nodded to her to continue pouring.

'A satisfactory wine. It has a dark, sensuous warmth.'

Lulled into over-confidence, Olympia set about pouring wine for the Master and his guests, with perhaps less care than she might wisely have exercised. When a tiny drop of the ruby liquid trickled down the neck of the bottle and fell on to the glossy, leather-clad leg of one of the Master's guests, the man cried out in fury:

'Careless little slut! See what you have done!'

'I'm so sorry, really I am!'

'Lick it up. Every drop,' commanded the Master.

The man seized Olympia by the hair and dragged her down on to her knees. As he held her there, she set about licking away the wine assiduously, making certain that every drop was gone.

But even when she had finished, the man was unsatisfied. He wanted more.

Reaching down, he unzipped his flies and took out his stiff member. Then he picked up his wine glass and deliberately emptied it over his lap, so that the crimson fluid cascaded over his hardness, settling in all its secret nooks and crannies like ruby-red dew.

'Every drop, Slave,' commanded the Master.

Olympia set to work with a will, lapping and sucking at the stranger's manhood with all the skill that she possessed. She must make him pleased with her, turn away his anger.

His hardness tasted good on her tongue, the mellow warmth of the wine mingling with the muskiness of his sex. Love-juice collected at the tip, slippery and with a hint of delicious saltiness. Aroused now beyond belief by fear and excitement, Olympia felt a familiar wetness between her thighs. She wished that he would lay her down on the ground, or across the table, even, and thrust into her, riding her to the blissful release she so desperately craved.

A few seconds later, and rather to Olympia's surprise, the stranger's phallus stiffened and then spurted its jets of opalescent pleasure on to her tongue. Some of the semen spattered her face, and some fell in heavy, white droplets on to the black leather of his trousers.

In a moment, she found herself surrounded as the men rose to their feet and towered above her. Their anger was palpable, and she felt her heart thumping with a strange, alien excitement. She did not want to feel desire, but here, in this bizarre and frightening place, all her defences were down. It was as though the desires within her were taking over her body, breaking down all the barriers of her will.

'See what you have done, Slave!' hissed the Master as she gazed up at him with a mixture of terror and desire.

'Punish her. Punish her now,' snarled one of the strangers, twisting Olympia's hair so that she winced with discomfort.

'Shall it be the whip; or the cat?'

Olympia bent her head in submission as they hauled her to her feet and bent her forwards over the tomb, holding her there in an iron grasp.

She tensed her body for the first blow, and when the pain came she was ready for it, and barely flinched. Enduring a few strokes of the cat was nothing, compared to the terror of holding the cobra close against her breast.

As the blows rained down upon her with a sensuous intensity, her mind drifted back to the time when she and Lars had made love in the snow on a Swedish mountain-side. Coming out of the sauna, their bodies exuding clouds of warm steam, they had run straight into the snow and thrown themselves down into the powder-soft whiteness. How it had burned; the cold seeming paradoxically as hot as naked flame on her hyper-sensitive flesh.

It was spring, and bright sunlight reflected off the hillside, dazzling them as they rolled and gasped in the snow. The muscular ski-ing instructor was used to such extremes of pleasure and discomfort, but Olympia was breathless and overcome by the intensity of the sensations. Her flesh seemed to burn, and yet she was cold, so very cold.

Lars entered her smoothly and skilfully, and by some miracle she was wet and ready for him. As they moved together in rhythmic fusion, the burning becoming a sensuous warmth, which in turn grew into the roaring furnace of passion. When at last she came, she had forgotten the cold, the snow, the discomfort, and surrendered utterly to the divine symphony of sensations.

Now, as the cat-o'-nine-tails rose and fell, marbling her skin with a rosy redness, Olympia was once again feeling that same delicious burning. A burning that seemed to centre on the soul and radiate outwards, making every nerve ending unbelievably sensitive. Her mind reeled and she no longer even thought of resistance, relaxing into the welter of sensations that washed over her like a turbulent, sparkling sea.

Voices surrounded her, weaving a net of sound, but she paid them no heed. Only the pleasure mattered; the pleasure of the moment.

Suddenly there was a new sensation – sharp and exquisite. For a moment she did not realise what was happening, and then recognition filtered into her mind. The handle of the cat-o'-nine-tails was sliding smoothly between her thighs, meeting the ready wetness of her womanhood. She thrust out her backside to meet the welcome invader, and sighed with delight as the warmth grew into a gentle pulsing, which in turn rose to a crescendo of excitement.

Pleasure. Pleasure at last.

'*Adieu*, sweet Slave.'

Olympia tried to free herself, but the chains held her fast, and she hung helplessly from the iron ring set into the old stone wall of the crypt.

'It is useless to struggle, my dear. The chains are strong, and I have locked the manacles securely.'

'But . . . what are you going to do to me now?'

'Do, my dear? Why, nothing at all! My work is done.'

The Master and his guests turned and walked towards the steps which led up out of the crypt, extinguishing the candles and torches as they went.

'Where are you going?'

There was no answer. At last, as the Master reached the bottom of the steps, there was only one candle left, illuminating the crypt with a feeble, unearthly light. The Master turned towards Olympia one last time.

'We must all confront our fears, my dear Slave. Use them, explore them; enjoy them.'

He lifted his hand and extinguished the final candle, plunging Olympia into utter blackness. Fear clutched at her heart as she heard the heavy door of the crypt bang shut. He was gone. And she was alone. Alone with her fears, and the cruel whispering of her darkest desires.

Chapter Twelve

*I*t was dark and bitterly cold in the crypt; and somewhere in the blackness Olympia could hear the scrabbling of night-creatures. She tried to calm herself, to tell herself that this was all part of the trial, but all the time a frantic voice within her was crying out: what if they leave you here? What if they forget about you and leave you in this terrible place, to die?

Time passed – she lost track of how long. Chill air circulated around her, raising goosepimples on her naked flesh. She was helpess. No one even knew she was here. Was this what her vanity and greed had brought her to, a lingering agony, surrounded by the age-old stench of death and decay?

Tears pricked her eyelids, but she would not let them fall. Even here, where no one could see her, Olympia Deschamps would not weep.

* * *

The sudden light dazzled her, and for many moments she blinked blindly in the lantern's beam.

'Light the candles and the torches.' The voice was unfamiliar, and Olympia hovered between hope and fear. Was this someone who had come to rescue her, or someone who had come only to continued her torment? Could it be that her trials were now at an end?

Brightness rose up slowly out of the black depths as the candles flickered back into life. Olympia found herself confronted by seven men – ordinary-looking men dressed in suits and ties, as if they were on their way to a business meeting. She recognised the magistrate among them, and the messenger, but the others were strangers.

'Good evening, Olympia.'

The seven men formed a semi-circle around her.

'Are you going to untie me now? My arms are pulled half out of their sockets.'

'All in good time, all in good time. The Légion has all the time in the world.'

'Have I . . . have I completed the challenges to your satisfaction?'

The Légionnaire smiled and nodded.

'*Mais oui, Mademoiselle Deschamps.* We have been most impressed with your ingenuity and enthusiasm. Your resilience, also, in the face of danger and fear. Your handling of the cobra, for instance – most impressive.'

'But it was not dangerous. You removed its fangs, surely?'

'*Mais non, ma chère Mademoiselle! Absolument non.* One bite from *Monsieur le cobre*, and you would have been no more.'

Olympia felt a slight sensation of nausea as she realised how close to death she had allowed herself to be placed.

'A Légionnaire never shirks danger, Olympia – I am sure your father told you that. Now, my dear, there is yet one more challenge for you to overcome before we can consider admitting you to the Légion.'

'Another challenge? But I was told that seven trials were all I needed to complete.'

'My dear Olympia, the entrance procedures are extremely rigorous, as I am sure you will appreciate. Before being admitted to the ranks of the Légion, all our candidates must satisfy us not only of their skill, vigour and endurance, but of their powers of self-denial.'

'This is your task, my dear,' explained the magistrate, coming forward out of the shadows and laying his hand thoughtfully upon her breast. 'We shall stimulate your body with all the skill and ingenuity at our disposal. But you, my dear, must resist us with all the powers within you. If you betray any sign of desire, the penalty shall be death. Are you willing?'

Olympia's head was reeling. How could this be? She had come so far, and still she had not escaped from the shadow of death! Fear tautened her belly, but she knew she must not fail now, at this final hurdle. There could be no going back.

'I am willing,' she replied. 'I am not afraid.'

Hands reached out to her; hands that had all the flames of lust within their fingertips. Hands that knew every corner of a woman's body, every way to awake her senses and inflame her desires. There

243

was no way to escape, no way to fend off their insistent caresses.

She bit her lip until it bled, knowing that she must show no sign of the raging torrent within her. Desire was welling up like a flood tide, threatening to burst its banks, to spill over, to engulf all in its path.

The words pounded in her head; death or denial, death or denial.

It was a cruel, impossible choice, and suddenly she knew what she must do. Opening her eyes, she screamed into the darkness beyond the flickering candlelight: 'Death! I choose death, if that is the penalty for pleasure! I will not deny my desires!'

Startled, the men drew back from her, taking their hands from her pulsating, yearning body. But she drew them back to her with a wild, glittering stare.

'Pleasure me before I die! I claim pleasure as my right.'

Their hands, their tongues, their subtle fingertips awoke a crescendo of passion within her as they cut her down and laid her across the granite slab of tomb. Aching with need, she unleashed her pleasure with groans and sighs that became piercing cries of anguished delight. Now, all that mattered was to reach that climax, that pulsing crescendo of pleasure. And she undersood that what the stranger had told her was true.

Desire – faceless, faithless desire – was all that mattered to her, here and now. Later, she would face the terrible consequences of her recklessness; but for now, desire would be her only *raison d'être*.

She abandoned herself to joy in the full knowl-

244

edge of what would then happen to her. The anticipation of retribution did not hold any terrors for her now, only the sweet understanding that, in a strange way, she had won.

She lay spreadeagled on the granite tomb for many long minutes, dazed and disoriented by pleasure. Then, to her amazement, they lifted her gently from the stone and set her on her feet, surrounding her with smiles and laughter.

The magistrate was first to speak.

'Allow me to offer you my sincerest congratulations, Mademoiselle Olympia.'

'Congra . . . what do you mean?'

'Mademoiselle, plainly you do not understand the full significance of what you have done. You see, *ma chère*, a true Légionnaire *always* puts desire before denial, even when the penalty is death. Your late father would have been very proud of you, Olympia.'

'You mean . . .?'

'*Oui, Mademoiselle*. Welcome to the Légion d'Amour, Légionnaire Deschamps.'

Relaxing on the plane to London, Olympia reflected on the events of the past few days. It had been an eventual week, all things considered. Soon she would be touching down at Heathrow, and Joachim would be there waiting for her, an oasis of blissful normality in this insane life which she had chosen for herself.

She played thoughtfully with the gold puzzle ring she now wore proudly on her right hand: the ring of the Légion d'Amour. And she recalled Joachim's last words to her before he left for London and his first big exhibition:

'You've taught me such a lot, *ma chère* Olympia. I was nothing before I met you – just a clumsy boy. But I feel I've still got so much more to learn from you.'

A smile played about her lips as she reflected on the truth of Joachim's words.

Now that she had the secret lore of the Légion d'Amour to guide her, Olympia Deschamps would be able to teach him anything a man could ever want to know.

Already published

NO LADY
Saskia Hope

30 year-old Kate dumps her boyfriend, walks out of her job and sets off in search of sexual adventure. Set against the rugged terrain of the Pyrenees, the love-making is as rough as the landscape. Only a sense of danger can satisfy her longing for erotic encounters beyond the boundaries of ordinary experience.

ISBN 0 352 32857 6

WEB OF DESIRE
Sophie Danson

High-flying executive Marcie is gradually drawn away from the normality of her married life. Strange messages begin to appear on her computer, summoning her to sinister and fetishistic sexual liaisons with strangers whose identity remains secret. She's given glimpses of the world of The Omega Network, where her every desire is known and fulfilled.

ISBN 0 352 32856 8

BLUE HOTEL
Cherri Pickford

Hotelier Ramon can't understand why best-selling author Floy Pennington has come to stay at his quiet hotel in the rural idyll of the English countryside. Her exhibitionist tendencies are driving him crazy, as are her increasingly wanton encounters with the hotel's other guests.

ISBN 0 352 32858 4

CASSANDRA'S CONFLICT
Fredrica Alleyn

Behind the respectable facade of a house in present-day Hampstead lies a world of decadent indulgence and darkly bizarre eroticism. The sternly attractive Baron and his beautiful but cruel wife are playing games with the young Cassandra, employed as a nanny in their sumptuous household. Games where only the Baron knows the rules, and where there can only be one winner.

ISBN 0 352 32859 2

THE CAPTIVE FLESH
Cleo Cordell

Marietta and Claudine, French aristocrats saved from pirates, learn their invitation to stay at the opulent Algerian mansion of their rescuer, Kasim, requires something in return; their complete surrender to the ecstasy of pleasure in pain. Kasim's decadent orgies also require the services of the handsome blonde slave, Gabriel – perfect in his male beauty. Together in their slavery, they savour delights at the depths of shame.

ISBN 0 352 32872 X

Forthcoming publications

OUTLANDIA
Georgia Angelis

At first, Iona Stanley longs for her temperate home of nineteenth century England. Shipwrecked on the remote South Sea island of Wahwu, she finds the exotic customs of the inhabitants alarmingly licentious. But her natural sensuality blossoms as she is crowned living goddess of the island. Her days are spent luxuriating in the tropical splendour, being worshipped by a host of virile young men. Suddenly, things don't seem so bad after all.

ISBN 0 352 32883 5

BLACK ORCHID
Roxanne Carr

The Black Orchid is a women's health club which provides a specialised service for its high-powered clients; women who don't have the time to spend building complex relationships, but who enjoy the pleasures of the flesh. One woman, having savoured the erotic delights on offer at this spa of sensuality, embarks on a quest for the ultimate voyage of self-discovery through her sexuality. A quest which will test the unique talents of the exquisitely proportioned male staff.

ISBN 0 352 32888 6